Treasures
of the Kingdom
Volume One

Starlight Publishing – Coeur d'Alene, Idaho

TREASURES OF THE KINGDOM
VOLUME ONE

© 2007 Starlight Publishing, Jan Finnamore, Rebekah Garvin
Coeur d'Alene, Idaho USA

Printed by Lulu.com
Hardcover and Softcover First Edition, January 2007

ISBN 978-0-6151-4562-4 (softcover)

ALL RIGHTS RESERVED
No part of this publication may be reproduced, stored in a retrieval system,
or transmitted, in any form or by any means--electronic, mechanical,
photocopying, recording, or otherwise--without prior written permission
from the author.

Layout and Design by
Jan Finnamore Rebekah Garvin

Cover Design by Rebekah Garvin

Stories compiled by Jan Finnamore and Rebekah Garvin
Treasure stories gleaned from the internet and historical books

Biblical texts taken from the New International Version and The Message

Personal stories of transformation contributed by Tracey Black, Jim Braman,
Gail Cary, Jan Finnamore, Chris Garvin, Rebekah Garvin, Katrin Jurdan, Fred
Pitzl, Tiffany Reynolds, Gary Taylor, Brenda, David and Mithril.

The personal testimonies and photographs printed here were used with
express written permission. This book was not printed or reviewed by
John Eldredge, nor is it in any way affiliated with the Ransomed Heart
Ministries.

Cover photo and other photos are from Photodisc stock photography.
Some of the photos were contributed by the writers and others were taken
by A Chance Encounter Photography.

For more books published through Starlight Publishing visit:
www.lulu.com/starlight. Contact us through Land of Iona's website at:
www.landofiona.com

Dedicated to:

THE TRINITY

in grateful celebration of Your relentless pursuit of our hearts.
Thank you...thank you...thank you! We'd be lost without You.

And to:

JOHN AND STASI ELDREDGE
AND THE RANSOMED HEART MINISTRY TEAM

who, through their own journeys and blazing desire to follow the
Wild Goose, have fought for so many of our hearts with epic truth
reclaimed, releasing us into the presence of our Wild God and
True Father. May our stories encourage you to continue invading
enemy territory. You are needed and play a very crucial role in
this War. Thank you for putting into words the movements of
our hearts.

Our lives have been transformed by Him and our vision will
never be the same because of your faithfulness to His call.

You are My Priceless Treasure

- God -

Disclaimer:

These stories were not written by professional writers, but by people on a journey. Please read them with grace.

Also, this book was compiled, edited and designed by the warrior hearts of two busy moms who believe the Trinity has invited them into an allied relationship for Kingdom advancement in these last days. So, it is during really late nights and really early mornings--between dishes, laundry, children, career, school and their own personal journeys that these moms who live on two opposite sides of the continent have heard the voice of God and moved upon it.

This book was not printed or reviewed by
John Eldredge, nor is it in any way affiliated with
Ransomed Heart Ministries.

CONTENTS

THERE IS MORE

No matter what you have known, no matter how precious your life with God has been to date, or how disappointed you've been and elusive he may have seemed . . . there is more available with God.

There is so much more. Now. In this life.

But to discover that "more," we must launch out into deep waters, leave what is familiar, search for new shores. We must learn to live in the rest of reality, which is to say, we must learn to see life spiritually, and we must take seriously the fierce battle for our hearts.

We must get our hearts back.

John Eldredge and Craig McConnell
from A Guidebook to *Waking the Dead*

Sing a new song
to the LORD!

Let the whole earth sing to the LORD!
Sing to the LORD; bless his name.

Each day proclaim the good news
that he saves.

Publish his glorious deeds
among the nations.

Tell everyone about the
amazing things he does.

Great is the LORD!

He is most worthy of praise!

– Psalm 96: 1-4 –

❦ ❦ ❦

INTRODUCTION

A lost pet, a lost engagement ring, a lost child...a lost treasure. We know the angst of something lost. We plaster the neighborhood with posters when our dog strays. We frantically search the house and retrace our steps when we discover our diamond has slipped from its post. And when we can't find our child? Terror fills our heart; life stops as we know it. We don't eat; we don't sleep; it's an all out search until the one who is lost, is found.

The Kingdom of Heaven has experienced loss as well. Jesus told a trio of parables of lost things: a lost sheep, a lost coin, a lost son, to help us understand God's heart toward us. He wanted us to know our hearts are the treasure of the Kingdom, and that He was on a dangerous and costly mission "to seek and to save that which was lost." (Luke 19:10)

Because of the Fall, and the Epic Battle that now rages between the Kingdom of Light and the Kingdom of Darkness, our hearts have known much loss and ruthless plundering from the Thief who comes to steal, kill and destroy. (John 10:10) But Christ's death, resurrection and accession stated God's clear intention. In no uncertain terms, God declared our value. We do not decide our own worth. He has stated what we are worth! And if we are to walk in faith, we must agree with Him. This pleases Him, and is a true expression of our belief in Him. He wants us to know beyond all shadow of a doubt, that our hearts are indeed greatly treasured by His heart. And He longs that we be found and completely restored to the glory He intended for us before the foundation of the world.

And it is important that we know God's heart on this, for lost things rarely know their value. A diamond mired in mud no longer sparkles. A shipwreck holding a multimillion-dollar cache does nothing to aid being found. A kidnapped or abused child often believes they are no longer loved, or worse, they deserve the horror that came their way. And a heart, lost, lies wounded, buried in lies by the Thief who whispers and shouts to our hearts, we are unlovely, worthless and despised. And so, many hearts are lost to God, weighed down by shame, guilt, sorrow and despair...feeling desperate and unloved...trapped in endless cycles of defeat. Many are lost to the abundant life that Jesus came to bring.

Ransomed Hearts-Our Story, Volume One is a collection of stories of lost hearts, found. And like Jesus long ago, Rebekah and I have tried to incorporate stories of buried treasure in a field, pearls of great price, lost shipwrecks...anything...to help our hearts capture a glimpse of God's heart --the Biggest Treasure Hunter of us all. He wants all of His Beloved Sons and Daughters back, with their hearts fully restored, ruling and reigning beside Him in all of their glory. Not one day, far away, but now. In this life. Here. Jesus stated, "I have come that you might have life, and have it more abundantly.". (Jn 10: 10) For He knows, that He is most glorified when we are most satisfied in Him. And as Saint Irenaeus said so long ago, "The glory of God is man fully alive." We agree. It is indeed.

To the King and His Kingdom...and to His Beloved Sons and Daughters!

– Jan Finnamore and Rebekah Garvin
December 2006

✿ ✿ ✿

EACH STORY MATTERS

Each of us has a story. It is our own story. It belongs to us, no one else. It is ours to write and share. As in any good story, there are many characters. In my story I am the main character. In your story, you are the main character. Each story is important. Each story matters.

Many of our stories overlap. I may be a character in some of your stories. Some of you may be characters in mine. As I am writing about my story, it may be necessary for me to include another character who played a critical role. This person may be you or someone you know. Sometimes a writer may change a name to provide anonymity to that person. That is okay, but not always possible. Sometimes we write about someone who has a specific position in our story which is impossible to disguise. Such as father, mother, brother, sister, son, daughter, etc. There are times when a difficult story must be told. It is then especially important to view life and stories in the way I have been describing.

You must remember that when I am telling my story, it is just that, mine. An event in my story involving another character may have been very critical to me, but may not have mattered at all to the other person. That other person may not remember the event at all. Or they may remember it very differently in their story. As you know from your close relationships, what is heard matters much more than what is said. Is that fair? It doesn't matter if it is fair or not. It just is. As I have discovered, some of the messages I received that impacted me the most were delivered without words.

We must remember that each of us has our own story to tell. When we write about someone who did us harm in our story, it is critical to remember that they also have their own story. This is critical for both writer and reader. Especially if the reader knows, or is, that other character. As the writer, I would have to say, "This is my story. It matters to me. I do not demand that you understand. I only ask that you allow me the freedom to have my own story, and that you allow me the freedom to tell it for the benefit of others."

– Chris Garvin

✴ ✴ ✴

❦ ❦ ❦

GUARD YOUR HEART

"Above all else, guard your heart"
– Proverbs 4:23–

We usually hear this with a sense of "keep an eye on that heart of yours," in the way you'd warn a deputy watching over some dangerous outlaw, or a bad dog the neighbors let run. "Don't let him out of your sight." Having so long believed our hearts are evil, we assume the warning is to keep us out of trouble.

So we lock up our hearts and throw away the key, and then try to get on with living. But that isn't the spirit of the command at all. It doesn't say guard your heart because it's criminal; it says guard your heart because it is the wellspring of your life, because it is a treasure, because everything else depends on it. How kind of God to give us this warning, like someone entrusting to a friend something precious to him, with the words: "Be careful with this–it means a lot to me."

– John Eldredge
Waking the Dead (pp. 207-208)

✿ ✿ ✿

FOUND: Treasure of David

Heart of a Lion

I have loved you from the beginning of time, and you will be with me forever.

I will thank you, LORD, with all my heart;
I will tell of all the marvelous things you have done.
I will be filled with joy because of you. I will sing praises
to your name, O Most High.

Psalm 9:1-2

FOUND:
TREASURE OF DAVID

Heart of a Lion

by David

I had not realized that there was much more work that God was doing and continues to do in my life until I began to write down my story. I recommend this exercise to everyone God has healed and freed and who needs and wants more.

My story is a story of failure, underachievement, betrayal, and heartache-beyond-measure, all set in a lifetime (54 years) of searching for life and the Giver-of-Life.

It is also a story of a rescue of a thirteen-year-old boy whose heart was dismissed for forty years.

I just finished "Sam's Year" a chapter in John Eldredge's most recent book *The Way of the Wild Heart*. The chapter is an incredible documentary on the initiation and coming of age of John's eldest son Sam.

The story of Sam's thirteenth year: the love and challenges of a father, the support of the community, and the acceptance by the men in his life, culminating in a celebration into manhood. An awesome guide for how to nurture, love, develop and mature a boy's heart. John uses this in his book to point out what God, our true Father, has intended for us men all along, and that it is still available, regardless of a person's age now.

My thirteenth year was a stark contrast to Sam's year and to what God had intended for me. I was born the fourth child of eight into a Catholic family. My mother came from a fairly well-to-do family and my dad from a family of poor farmers. I never knew my dad's dad; he had died before I was born. His mother was a very kind woman who was the only family member that I can remember in my childhood who loved me for me.

I remember once falling asleep in her arms; I'd had an earache and she was holding me and rocking me; I was about five then. The reason I can remember this so clearly is because this was the only time in my childhood that I can remember love; someone cared.

With eight kids to feed and clothe, my dad worked. And mom—she seemed always angry. I think her anger was partly due to going from having everything to having nothing.

Yelling was easiest for her to get us to behave. I did not know tenderness. And the thought of someone caring for my heart? It was never seen.

I cannot remember one time in all my growing up of a single moment alone with my Dad. Not one. Yes, he would play football and baseball with the (five) boys; take us to lakes, morel mushroom hunting and parks. But not once was it ever just he and I, not once....

My siblings didn't make life easy for me either; with eight of us competing for affections, and very little to be shared, it is understandable. None of us received what we needed when we needed it the most.

My thirteenth year was most especially difficult. Dad had lost a good job and we had to move away from a school where I was accepted (and sought after) by my teacher (Sister

Mary Marie) and to my surprise the entire seventh-grade class. I was "somebody" for the first time in my life.

The news that we were leaving was devastating and I remember crawling into a rolled up carpet where I hid and cried for a very long time. I knew that my life, the little that I had, would never be the same.

We moved to an old farmhouse that was cold, dark and damp and matched the mood of the rest of my childhood. I lived in a room with three other brothers and had to share a bed with one of them.

Sister Marie had sent me a letter a few months after we had moved and my mother embarrassed me with it during supper. Sister Marie had said how she and the class missed me and that God had something very special for my life with Him. My Mother's comment: "Yea right." My Dad? No comment, no defense, no support. Nothing.

Anger, deep anger came next.

I was teased by my brothers and sisters, and one day, I grew so angry that I took a claw hammer to a door upstairs. Dad's response was to have the brothers hold me down until I calmed down.

Yep, that was it.

Didn't take me to the woodshed, didn't take me aside to talk to me, nothing. No, worse than nothing, I was dismissed; no one cared.

The things that I did care about during this time of my life began to be removed. It seemed that it wasn't enough that I was dismissed, but the assault on my heart reached considerably deeper.

The farmer whose house we were renting had a cottage behind our house and his daughter and new husband lived there. She was very beautiful and she loved to talk and be with us. She was a gleam of light during this dark age. But she died of a complication with her pregnancy before spring of that year.

During that same time, a neighbor had accused our pet collie of chasing sheep. Dad had us take her with him to the back forty, had us dig a hole and put her in it – tail wagging and all, and he shot her in front of us with a twelve gauge.

We finished burying her.

Come to find out, the neighbor tagged the wrong dog; it wasn't Queenie that chased their sheep after all.

My best friend, and really only friend, was a neighboring farm boy who had polio. He got around pretty well, and we would hike his dad's property, camp out, and hang out on his farm. I would help with the work at times; they had milking cows, sheep, chickens and crops to manage.

One day my friend's dad told me to get the hell off his farm. I didn't understand; but he insisted and he never gave me a reason. Even my friend couldn't explain. I think something might have gotten stolen–I don't know. I never got the whole story.

Anyway, what was stolen from me was my friend.

Thirteen years old, no real friends, most of what I cared about removed. A mother who showed no kindness, mercy, or beauty; a father who appeared to not care–he was too busy and lacked the heart to know how to go after my heart.

He never went after my heart. Not then, not ever.

The next five years I lived in a house with nine others, yet felt like an orphan: alone, angry, irrelevant.

Dismissed.

What choices are left for a wounded animal, placed into a small pen, and left alone? Of course all I had was myself and survival was up to me. I had no one walking with me through this time; no one to explain how to handle all the hurt and pain; no one to explain what I was supposed to do with "wet dreams," acne, a growing body; no one to walk me across this threshold of boy-to-man.

No one.

I married the first girl I dated and had sex with. I was

married three days after I turned eighteen-years-old. I was married by a priest who my mom hooked me up with as a mentor during my teenage years. Turns out, my mom was using me to spend time with the priest and had an affair with him (learned this many years later).

I joined the military when I was eighteen, and took my pregnant wife to the Pacific Northwest. This was my ticket out of my house.

I had dreamed, since thirteen, of running away. One time, I almost jumped onto a slow train with only a pocket full of change.

I only stayed in the military until after the Viet Nam War. During that time I worked with a girl who was a "born again Christian" and she talked to me about God. I liked listening to her because she was attractive and cared.

My anger didn't leave when I left the mid-west. It came with me. And when I decided to "give my heart to the Lord," the anger was only driven underground ... for awhile.

During my twenties and early thirties I went to a local community church and that seemed to take care of the "God" thing in my life.

What I really liked was the hiking and mountain

David and his wife Brenda

climbing with the guys. This gave me confidence and seemed to be a way of handling anger, but it also opened the door for using this new confidence to have affairs and seek the affirmation I never got in my youth.

I had two sons from my first wife. They became orphans at the ages of eight and fourteen when I divorced her.

I had attempted to go after their hearts; I certainly spent considerably more time with them then my father had with me.

But it was not the time that mattered; it was the knowing how to go after their hearts–which I didn't, because I didn't get that either.

They are now twenty-nine and thirty-five with their own set of problems–mostly not understanding the way of the heart.

I was into bars, nightlife, some drugs, gambling–anything to cover up a failed marriage, failed fatherhood, a failed life!

When Brenda and I met, our relationship was unlike anything I had known up till then. We had both come from failed marriages and a strict upbringing.

She was an ex-JW and I was an ex-Catholic (you got to love God's sense of humor), and we both were scared to death of dealing with this with our mothers.

What we realized early was that though we were not walking with God, He put on our hearts to get our lives in order; and though we could not fix the past, the future could be different. I couldn't reach my sons any longer in a direct way, but I could give them an example of a better life. We went "church hopping" for a few years, knowing that God needed to be in our lives; or at least this is how we saw it. He was the one pressing the issue, we just didn't know it.

Over the next decade Brenda and I got married, and we tried to help the boys as best we could. The oldest son got married early and now has five children with another one the way—he is struggling financially.

The youngest son has already been married, divorced, and in and out of a self-help support institution for gambling and other problems. He is currently living out of the back of his (just-on-the-verge-of-falling-apart) truck and a couple of states are after him for child support.

In the middle of facing all of these problems, I lost the only mentor I had ever known–my boss at work. He really wasn't a mentor from his point of view, but I looked up to him from mine.

Anyway, he retired and not long after that, a deep anger returned. I was angry at work, angry with my sons, and the anger even threatened my second marriage.

It was Christmas of 2003, and through a suggestion by someone she trusted, Brenda gave me the book *Wild at Heart* by John Eldredge.

After "playing" church and seeking answers for decades, here was something new and more real with more hope than anything I had ever known.

The idea of brokenness and being held captive, I understood ... my life was a text book example. But the idea that Christ's real mission was to come after me and fix all of that? That he wanted to initiate me, mature me, and fix the past so that I can have life, real life in this lifetime?

That my heart is good, that I can live and be a part of a larger story; that I am invited to fight back at the enemy who has caused all of the death and destruction in my life, and fight for my sons, and my grandchildren?

I wanted to hear more and know more so I bought all of John's books, CDs, DVDs. And then the next year I talked Brenda into changing our vacation plans from the Oregon coast to Colorado–there was a conference, a sort of a spiritual boot camp that I wanted to attend.

The two weeks that we spent in the Frazier Valley in Colorado, and especially the four days I spent at Crooked

Creek Ranch in September of 2004, profoundly and eternally changed the direction of my life.

Entering the ranch was like stepping into a spiritual sanctuary. When I was fearful to make this commitment to go to this conference, God softly assured me that if I would just show up, He would meet me there.

He showed up!

It wasn't even ten minutes into the first meeting and my tears were flowing. I think I wore out a half dozen of those big blue handkerchiefs over the next four days.

Discovering wounds, healing, getting in touch with the message of the heart that John and his team worked hard to present to the 400 guys, came immediately for me.

I had heard that for some "getting it" or seeing their wounds came hard, and for some not even until some time after the gathering. Not me.

I had had nearly fifty-three years of defenseless battle to soften me up. Nope, I got it, and got it, and got it ... and am still getting it. Jesus keeps coming for more; even as I am writing this story, He is touching, healing, and freeing more areas in my life.

One of the first things we were asked at the boot camp to write down, and to provide an answer for, was a question from God: "What do you want from me?"

I had never journaled in my life, so this was the first thing in my new journal (the blank book they gave us at boot camp).

Here is my answer that I wrote that first day: "To understand the language of Your heart, to love You and no longer look at You as a taskmaster."

Saturday morning at Crooked Creek, after a day and half of emotional visits to the wounds in my past, I was invited by the Maker of the universe to join him high up on a hill to watch the sunrise with him.

I loved the hike and learned to walk with Him in these

mountains at that time of year with aspens changing, mountain vistas, seeing deer and a fox.

This was a practical lesson for me in how to "walk with God." I just went for a walk and He joined me.

When I reached a high point, I was a bit out of breath, but the sun had not yet peaked over the ridge to the east. I was fifty-two years old, not in the best shape, but I felt like a boy.

As the sun shot its first ray over the range, it looked like a diamond, and as it grew higher I could feel the warmth immediately.

In my heart He spoke to me and told me the past was over; that this was a new day and He gave me a glimpse of the future of His Church, His People and the new "Promised Land." He told me that I had a place and part to play.

I understood the heart of Joshua when he, along with Caleb insisted that the land "can be taken." And I know that God has placed that spirit in my heart now.

During the session at boot camp, when we were invited to ask God who we are to Him, what our true name was, I went for a walk and ended up in a stand of aspens. In my heart's eye I saw a lion walking and moving between the trees.

"Is that my name, Father? Lion?"

No. He said. *What is it that moves the lion?* He asked.

"His heart."

Yes, Heart-of-a-lion.

I was reminded that as His heart moves me, He wanted me to know that my heart moves Him.

Those four days in the spiritual sanctuary of the Crooked Creek Ranch were nothing like I had ever experienced in my entire life. I didn't get to know many guys there because God reminded me many times that we weren't there for each other; this was an invitation to walk with Him.

Just recently, I spent time with a guy who was in the same bunk house as me (two years prior), and it took us a good part of a day to figure that out. Yes, we were in the same room for three nights. He had much that same reaction I did, that he was there with God and it was all about Him.

As we got closer to the end of our time at boot camp, a terrible fear came across me. My life had been so hard and painful; I never wanted to leave that place.

They could just bury me up on the mountain somewhere and that would be fine with me.

One of the assignments that John gave us on the last day was to go walk with God, be alone with Him and ask Him what our deepest fear was after leaving this place before "going back into the matrix," as John put it.

I was sad on my walk. I was walking with a new joy in my heart, but sad to consider leaving the camp.

So I asked God, "What am I afraid of?"

And for awhile He was silent, and so I just walked and soaked in the brilliant blue sky, the mountains, birds, changing aspens, endless forests. I sat down on a log for awhile and just soaked it all in; admiring Him for such an awesome creation.

Then I remembered the assignment, and the pain returned. Why am I afraid to leave, why am I fearful?

And as I walked slowly back, God asked me a question: *What do you think these mountains, trees, animals, sky, my creation thinks of you walking in their midst?*

In a simple question He reminded me who I am, my place as His image bearer, and my role over His creation. My whole life I was intimidated by deep woods, high mountains, wild animals and places. But no longer.

I am David, Heart-of-a-lion, a beloved son of the Lion of Judah.

When I go hiking and climbing now, I am still awed at His awesome creation, but when I walk among it, I feel a welcoming like my surroundings are saying to me, "Your highness, thank you for your presence here. We are here for you."

Not long after boot camp God gave me a promise and a

verse. I wrote what he said to me in my journal: *I will restore all that was lost when you were twelve. I have loved you from the beginning of time, and you will be with me forever.*

And the verse He showed me came from Psalm 90:15, Moses' request from God, "Make us glad for as many days as you have afflicted us, for as many years as we have seen trouble."

It has been over two years since I first learned to walk with Him and since he gave me my true name. And, oh what a time it has been.

"Glad" can't even begin to express the time since then. Yes, glad and much, much more. It has been more healing, yes, but He has been teaching me how to lead others to His healing.

I was able to go to Frontier Ranch a year later to learn more about the masculine journey and to gain more understanding of how to apply "walking with Him," the work of the Holy Spirit, healing, and spiritual warfare. Not just to gain knowledge, but He showed up and took me through (walked with me again in the woods) the meaning of "beloved son" and, showed me where I faced evil and what was part of a major battle that resulted in a stronghold being shattered and men's hearts being released and freed.

I also realized God wanted to give me a "David's Year." It actually started the day that I retired when Brenda drove to the Spokane Valley to the Sportman's Warehouse and bought me fly fishing gear for my retirement.

God taught me to fish, something I missed and always wanted to do. He provided funding for a piano and I just started to learn, something else I missed. And my biggest dream as a child was to learn to fly! I have a flight physical scheduled for end of December and if I pass that, ground school starts in January or February with opportunities to do in-flight training late winter or early spring.

The foundation that I should have gotten at thirteen is

now being re-built (Isaiah 58:12). I am looking forward to what He is going to do over the next ten months; building a foundation for the "next" forty years.

I know it seems a little selfish, but as John said that thirteenth year sets the tone for the rest of a boy's life . . . as you know I missed that part my life.

And I also no longer see God as a "taskmaster." I have learned to love Him deeply, and here is what He has taught me about the "language of His heart:"

> It is the language of love
> It pursues me my entire life
> It asks for entry but will not force
> It carries with it abundant life
> If defines "good"
> It is trustworthy
> It is pure
> It holds me spellbound

He also continues to add to my name, in a way to remind me who I am in Him. I have come a long way from the thirteen-year old who was all but abandoned, whose name at the time could be Failure, Underachiever, Loser, Lost and Unloved.

And so He asks me occasionally, *Who are you?*

My answer:

> I am David, Heart-of-a-Lion,
> A beloved son of the Lion of Judah.
>
> I was born the fourth child of eight of Donovan,
> I am the father of two sons, grandfather to six,
> Husband to Brenda, a daughter of the True

Light, and a gift from Him.

I have been born again into the Kingdom of
Heaven; now a loyal subject of the King of
Kings who ransomed His life for mine,
who conquered death and ascended to His
throne giving me life, power, and authority to
fight at His side.

I am a warrior with a good heart, free and
in the service of the Commander of Angel
Armies.

I am a Knight in the Fellowship of His heart.

I am David, Heart-of-a-Lion,
A beloved son of the Lion of Judah.

THE KINGDOM OF HEAVEN IS LIKE ...

A DIVER LOOKING
FOR TREASURE

Curiously, my quest for sunken treasure began in a small bookshop on the Galerie de la Reine, Brussels. I was nineteen and studying political science at the university.

Intrigued by a paperback book illustrating deep-sea divers wrestling a chest of gold coins from an old ship, I picked up the book and thumbed through its tales of sunken Spanish galleons, gold doubloons, and silver pieces of eight.

I was spellbound. I bought the book.

From that moment my political career was stillborn, my destiny set. I quit school to chase golden rainbows.

Childish? Perhaps. A dream? Definitely. But it was a dream that would become a lifestyle, luring me to all the oceans in search of gold-laden galleons and East Indiamen, 18th-century warships, and World War II booty.

That very summer I set out on my first treasure hunt, and although I found many wrecks, it would be 15 years later before I found my first treasure.

Compared with fiction, real treasure hunts can be terribly dull. They consist mainly of divers probing underwater with unromantic coal shovels or airlifts five or six punishing hours a day, month after month, year after year. Treasure divers endure muddy water, bad weather, tricky and dangerous currents, and often that cold, cold water. Still, I enjoy it more than anything else.

The cold and other problems are only a challenge. It's no fun to climb the easy slope, is it? And I enjoy the physical labor, balanced by the intellectual

research that is the basis of any successful dive.

But best of all, each time I go down I am as thrilled as the first time I strapped on tanksI become another animal, with new eyes and new limbs. I sense and feel different things when I enter that underwater fantasy land bathed in murky green.

Even during the disappointment of finding worthless wrecks I returned from each day's work exhausted and empty handed but gloriously happy. For I was doing exactly what I wanted. I valued my new found freedom and longed to continue diving. Those years were the best in my life.

Except for all the years since then. For in addition to the many intangible joys of diving, I'll never forget the thrill of finding my first sunken cache of gold, after 15 years of searching.

I had spent more than 600 hours digging in the dusty archives of five countries, seeking precise details about the Spanish Armada

ship Girona which sank in 1588
laden with treasure. The water
was rough and icy when we arrived
in 1967. We dove anyway, and the
hours of patient research paid
off.

Within an hour we found
Girona's grave, in 30 feet of
water. Not a splinter of the hull
remained, but cannonballs and brass
guns pointed the way to the first
Armada wreck ever discovered. We
soon found scattered pieces of
coins, tarnished by centuries of
immersion.

I started digging in a small
mound of sand, and there, gleaming
before my eyes, lay a few links of
gold chain, untouched by corrosion
that marked our other finds. I
was neither shocked nor stunned at
finding my first sunken treasure,
but felt a peaceful sense of
fulfillment.

This multimillion cache of
gold, gems and artifacts meant I
could continue diving.

Today, after many more
finds, I still seekand respect
those grande dames of history. My

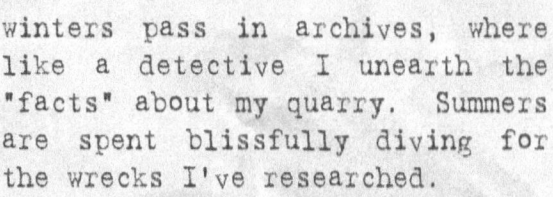

winters pass in archives, where
like a detective I unearth the
"facts" about my quarry. Summers
are spent blissfully diving for
the wrecks I've researched.

With me, treasure diving
is not just a hobby or even an
occupation; it is a way of life.
And I am very happy.

I suppose I could have been
successful in a more commonplace
occupation. But I'd have wasted
a good part of my life. And why?
I'm rich in what I value good
memories.

My only regret is that I
waited so long before hunting down
Girona.

Why didn't I start chasing
rainbows sooner?

Robert Stenuit 1974
<u>Undersea Treasures</u>
National Geographic Society

42

FOUND: Treasure of Brenda

A Maiden, Pure and Fair

I am yours . . . forever

But you, O LORD, are a shield around me, my glory, and the one who lifts my head high. I cried out to the LORD, and he answered me from his holy mountain.

Psalm 3: 3-4

FOUND:
TREASURE OF BRENDA

A Maiden, Pure and Fair

by Brenda

Once upon a time there was an innocent, young maiden who lived in a world full of love and laughter. She spent her days playing with her animals, reading with her mother, and talking with her grandfather.

One day, at the tender age of five, evil entered into her life, captured her and locked her away in a dark dungeon.

I am here to tell you my story of how love prevails over evil if you will let love in.

I was raised on a farm in Wyoming, the baby of six children. I spent a lot of time alone as a child, as my siblings are five to eleven years older than I am. My mom and I developed a great bond between us, as we spent a great deal of time together while my siblings attended school.

My oldest sister, Jocelyn, babysat a boy named Larry and his sister Donna during the summer, while she was out of school. Larry was a couple of years older than I was, and

Donna was one year younger than me.

One day, Larry, Donna and I were by the river playing in grove of Elm trees, when Larry began to touch me in places that were forbidden. He threatened to tell my parents that it was my idea if I told anyone about being molested. As an innocent five-year old, I believed him and kept my mouth shut, as he molested not only me, but also his own sister, day after day.

Later that same year, my world was once again rocked, as my sister Jocelyn ran away from home. I was devastated, as she and I were very close, even though she was eleven years my senior.

Mom went into a deep depression and had a nervous breakdown, leaving my dad, who worked two jobs, to care for five children and his father by himself.

I remember feeling abandoned and unloved, as two of the people I trusted most just checked out of my life. My ability to trust was shattered and I decided that I didn't need anyone.

Throughout my years at school, Larry would walk by me and hold his hand out, meaning that he wanted money to keep quiet about our "little secret." I knew that telling my parents would have meant severe chastisement and that my life would have been hell on earth as my parents, especially my mother was very strict. Larry knew that my grandfather gave me change, so I would give that to him.

As we grew older, I started working after school, as he wanted more money than a handful of Grandpa's change.

I will never forget the day of sweet peace when he finally graduated from high school, and I never saw or heard from him again. I buried that whole part of my life deep into the recesses of my heart and soul.

After I graduated from high school, I married the first guy I really ever dated. My parents were very strict, and I was not allowed to date until I was eighteen-years old.

I know now that I was taking my question to Adam, "Am I lovely?" That question was not answered, and after a horrible three-year marriage, we divorced.

Once again I sought solace, for my ever burning question, "Am I lovely," in Adam, and time after time, I never received the answer to that question.

David and Brenda

I then found other false lovers such as cigarettes, food and alcohol as a salve for my broken heart and yearning soul.

I met my current husband in 1986. It was love at first sight! We both had been married before, so it took us seven years to finally get married. We both had wounds from our lives, and tried to anesthetize the pain with cigarettes, gambling, and alcohol, to no avail.

One day, my sister Jocelyn showed up at my house with a new boyfriend named Larry. My world was once again rocked, as all of those memories I had so carefully locked away came flooding out. It was a torrent of emotions that I could not control.

I rarely cried, but it seemed that crying was all I did.

As a nurse, I knew about repression and I knew that the names Jocelyn and Larry had opened up that carefully sealed part of my heart. I had no idea what to do next. It certainly affected my marriage and I wanted to kill Larry for the pain he had caused me all those years ago, and was causing me again.

One day, the doctor I work for told me about a book that I just had to get for my husband. He had gone to a men's retreat the weekend before and came back filled with hope.

He told me to get the book *Wild at Heart* by John Eldredge. It was close to Christmas 2003, so I bought the book for my husband as a gift. That was the beginning of a wonderful journey for both of us.

We both read *Wild at Heart* and soon after had a complete library of all of John's books. We couldn't get enough of the hope and healing that God offers us.

Since learning how to walk with God, I have been healed of many things, including being molested as a child. I have forgiven Larry for his part in it, as I realize that Satan took him out at a tender age also, and that it was not his fault.

I have forgiven my mom and my sister for not rescuing me, as Satan was busy taking them out as well. Looking back on the whole situation, Satan was busy taking out my whole family.

Because of the healing God has granted me, I am able to talk about my past and I am able to help other women who come into my clinic who have had similar things happen to them. I offer hope to them by telling them what God had done for me and letting them know that they don't have to go through this alone.

I have also been healed from cigarettes, gambling, alcohol and food, as I have found my True Love and I don't need the false lovers any more. The peace I feel in my heart knowing that God loves me and does not blame me for what happened is overwhelming. I know that He finds me Captivating, and that is all that matters to me.

I enjoy photography and music, and am always eager to see what God is going to show me that day. Playing the guitar and the bass guitar allows me to express how I feel about Him, and every song I play, I play with abandonment for Him. When I am walking in His nature, I am reminded of the orange juice commercial where the little girl is sitting by her dad watching the sun go down and she says, "Do it again daddy."

That is how I feel when I am walking with Him and he shows me something spectacular. "Do it again Daddy!" He never fails me, He never abandons me, and He never stops loving me.

Once upon a time, there was a young maiden who lived in a beautiful castle that over looked the ocean to one side and majestic mountains on the other side. It was surrounded by a meadow filled with wild flowers and groves of Aspen and pine trees. She was Captivating and her lover was Wild at Heart and they lived happily ever after....

A ROYAL RING
FOUND IN A FIELD

It was lost for 650 years. No one knew it was lost. No one was looking for it.

They'd plowed the fields on the edge of Delamere Forest in Cheshire, England hundreds of times throughout the centuries, and no one had ever come across it or even had any idea it was there.

Until one rainy morning in 2002 when John Wood, a retired tool engineer from Manchester and amateur treasure hunter, asked if he could swing his metal detector through the newly ploughed field.

"Sure, but it isn't likely you'll

find anything." He'd been told.

Within two minutes his detector
gave a small signal and John dug up
what a friend later described as
"looking like one of those gifts
from a fairground."

On cleaning the ring, John found
the inscription *loyaute sans fin*
(loyalty without end), the letter
E engraved three times with three
stars, and, on either side of the
diamond, the two initials V and A.

At first the ring was believed to be
a love token and the Government's
treasure valuation committee
concluded it was 14th century and
worth only 3,000 pounds.

But John felt sure there was
something muchmoresignificant about
the ring and asked a specialist to
research the initials--to crack the
engraved code.

Jacob Van Artevelde, a wealthy
Flemish textile manufacturer
was Edward III's closest ally,

confidant and godfather to the king's children. And Delamere Forest was known to be one of the king's favorite hunting grounds.

"I can't tell you how rare this ring is. Diamonds were vary rare for the time. The goldwork is exquisite and, historically, we are potentially dealing with a royal ring." The researcher told John.

Setting a diamond that would have traveled the Silk Route from India to Europe was such a great rarity in 14th century Britain during the Hundred Years War, that only the wealthiest of the royals would have ever owned such a ring.

It is believed the ring was commissioned by Edward III as a gift to one of his most loyal supporters, Jacob Van Artevelde, bearing the initials of each friend. No one knows how the ring was lost, only that it has been found.

On June 15, 2006, a tiny 650-year-
old gold and diamond ring found
in a field by an amateur treasure
hunter fetched 84,000 pounds $149,
967.00 at auction.

✤ ✤ ✤

FOUND: Treasure of Jim Braman

Knight of Light

I am your Beloved and you are Mine.

I prayed to the LORD, and he answered me,
freeing me from all my fears. Those who look to him for help
will be radiant with joy; no shadow of shame will darken their
faces. I cried out to the LORD in my suffering, and he heard
me. He set me free from all my fears.
For the angel of the LORD guards all who fear him, and he
rescues them. Taste and see that the LORD is good.
Oh, the joys of those who trust him!

Ps. 34:4-8

FOUND:
TREASURE OF JIM BRAMAN

A Desperate Love

by Jim Braman

Let me introduce myself.

I am Don Quixote...Cervantes medieval knight who loved Dolcinea "pure and chaste from afar" and was on a mission to restore nobility and honor throughout the land–the impossible dream.

I use this mythic name as a reflection of my life, inspiring me to the same nobility and honor as I live out my calling in Jesus who has now become 'my life.'

Until the year 2000 I considered myself to be a pretty good guy. For twenty-five years I'd been a daily Bible reader and faithful church attendee. I'd also lead several small group Bible discussions over the years and made many 'sacrifices' for the kingdom of God.

I was making good money, had a big house, attended a big energetic church and was the father of two happy, lovable children and husband of a caring mother and wife for seventeen years.

In spite of all that something was missing. The busyness of life and the 'tyranny of the moment' were squeezing what was truly important out of my life.

I had a good beginning with God in 1975. While in college I began to read the Bible and fell in love with God, but over the years the values of the church and my upbringing began crowding him out.

"You're only worth what you produce . . . " was the message I was listening to. I was NOT accomplishing the 'great things' I was told and felt I should. I was not performing or measuring up as expected.

My relationship with God was not 'big' enough or real enough to stand on its own. I was trying to 'produce fruit' and become spiritually successful through careful application of just the right balance of good deeds, church service, family activity and my devotional life.

I was 'performing' my life before his eyes . . . not walking through it with him. My formulaic approach to life was failing, and even though there was still an underlying energy from the dream I once had, I had no clue what to do with it.

I had a great beginning filled with joy and adventure. But it was slowly ebbing away . . . eroding before my own eyes.

All this was intensified after I lost my job in 1998.

I was making a six figure income and in order to 'make ends meet' I had to weave several temporary jobs together at the same time to maximize my income. It was a losing battle and I knew we would have to move either to another city with a comparable job opportunity or to a lower income neighborhood.

As unstable and chaotic as things were, there was a part of me that liked the challenge. It was a distraction–however scary–from the inner spiritual turmoil I was in and allowed me to show myself as a hard worker . . . undaunted in the face of financial upheaval.

Eventually though, the deeper void returned. I tried numbing it again with intense spurts of religious activity and working harder, but it was never enough.

Slowly, things began to creep back into my life. Temptations and

Jim Braman

testing from years ago I thought were gone. Strange new ones came on top of those as well, and before long I found myself going down an adrenaline boosting path of empty adventure that led to crossing boundaries that in my wildest dreams I could not have imagined ever struggling with.

Finally, on February fifteen of the year 2000 everything I knew was blown away. I was confronted with my sin (the details of which are so twisted that, for a time, I was asked not to come to church), shortly after that I was asked to leave the house.

In spite of many tears and much remorse I could find no answer from God or man as to why I did what I did or how I got to that point.

I lived in four different places that first year, including a field behind a school for a few nights. To make matters worse the matrix of hourly jobs I had so cleverly woven was coming unraveled and my debts were beginning to mount.

During those first few months on my own I screamed and cried so hard that on one occasion my nose began to bleed. I prayed and fasted and spent hundreds of borrowed dollars on counselors and books. I enrolled in several groups and courses, but nothing was giving me the answers I was looking for.

I was spiritually bankrupt.

My whole soul needed resurrection . . . my entire existence from ground up. Everything I thought I knew about being spiritual was out the window . . . poof.

I knew nothing. Nothing about sin, nothing about myself, and most of all, I didn't know God.

Although many people have dramatic moments when the 'lights come on,' the answers and changes I was looking for came very gradually and without fanfare.

I began to go on weekend retreats to the mountains to try to find God and myself . . . possibly for the first time.

I came across *The Sacred Romance* by Brent Curtis and John Eldredge and the pages lifted me out of the hopelessness of the lifeless dutiful religion I had experienced for much of my life.

The words and music of Michael W. Smith also helped bring the tears of grief and healing that were aching to be shed.

Then came *Journey of Desire* and the other Eldredge books which continued to solidify the new outlook and identity I

Jim Braman

was being given by God.

After three years I now have a band of brothers that is pursuing a truly free walk with Christ . . . the same as the brothers from ages past in Iona that I read about in Waking the Dead.

As I look back now, I truly believe God heard every scream and cry . . . as useless as it all felt. Since that time my life has mostly been about healing and rebuilding. But more than that, it's been about truly falling in love with God, my Creator and Father, in a deep and passionate way.

I now have a marriage relationship with God that has been built through hours and hours of walks and reading and journaling. Through trips (dates) to the mountains and through sleepless nights. Just lying in bed thinking about him. Asking him questions and listening for his answers. Hearing his voice in everyday life events.

I wear a Hebrew wedding ring on my right hand now to remind me of my marriage to Jesus. I have discovered how deeply valued I am to God regardless of performance, and that He loves me more than I ever imagined. Knowing Him is worth every minute I have. These words of Peter the Apostle now have a meaning they never had before:

Though you have not seen Him, you love Him; and are filled with an inexpressible and glorious joy, for you are receiving the goal of your faith, the salvation of your souls.

I Peter 1:8

Although the consequences of my sin continue and are severe (divorce, bankruptcy, and loss of career), my desire is not to 'get back' to anything but rather to simply walk with God going forward wherever he seems to be leading.

My whole purpose now is to help other people see their

desperate need for God and wake up from the sleep of this world before it's too late.

Like Don Quixote, I want to help people find the true nobility and beauty God created in their souls; to fight the unbeatable foe by investing my heart, my soul, my mind, and my strength, my time, my money, my decisions, and my imagination in Jesus. Loving pure and chaste from afar. This is my quest, to follow that Star.

No matter how hopeless. No matter how far. Until I'm finally home with Him . . . forever.

✽　✽　✽

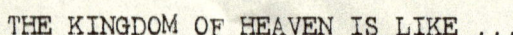

THE KINGDOM OF HEAVEN IS LIKE ...

LOST SHIPS IN THE GREAT LAKES

THE LEXINGTON (1847)
lies undisturbed at the bottom
of Lake Erie. Her treasure is
estimated somewhere between $70K-
$300K.

THE SUPERIOR (1856)
is hidden in the depths of
Lake Superior. Her gold and
silver valued to be $40K.

THE PEWABIC (1865)
sank in Huron. She holds $1
million in gold and $700K in
copper.

THE CHICORA (1895)
disappeared to the floor of Lake
Michigan. She carried $50K in
gold.

❦ ❦ ❦

FOUND: Treasure of Jan Finnamore

Fairytale Princess

Come be with me!

I am overwhelmed with joy in the LORD my God!
For he has dressed me with the clothing of salvation and draped
me in a robe of righteousness. I am like a bridegroom in his
wedding suit or a bride with her jewels. The Sovereign LORD
will show his justice to the nations of the world. Everyone
will praise him! His righteousness will be like a garden in
early spring, filled with young plants springing up everywhere.

Isaiah 61:10-11

FOUND:
TREASURE OF JAN FINNAMORE

Love has Called to Me

by Jan Finnamore

Come be with Me! Come be with Me!
Come be with Me!

It was 6 am. The alarm clock said I had another hour to sleep, but I was being roused out of bed.

Come be with Me! Come be with Me!

"Okay! I'm coming!"

I could hardly get down the stairs without feeling hurried, compelled.

As I walked into the kitchen and headed toward the coffee I heard, *I have a table prepared for you.*

Instantly, He had my attention. You see, several months prior as I had been praying for a friend of mine, the Lord had shown me an image in my mind of this friend sitting at a gorgeous banquet table–white linen table clothes, wine goblets, platters piled high with fruits, cheeses and meats.

My friend had dined to satisfaction, put his feet up and

pushed back his chair, his sword was lying at his side in the grass and Jesus was standing behind him anointing his head. It was a beautiful scene. So serene.

But then I noticed the banquet table was set in the midst of a *Lord of the Rings* style battlefield, yet the area surrounding the immediate table was protected as if it were in a glass dome. The battle was raging all around the table, and although the battle could still be seen, there was peace, blessing and abundance at the table.

I have a table prepared for you.

"Lord, you have a table like that prepared for me?"

Yes.

I then felt nudged to find a picture from an old, forgotten magazine I'd held on to from ten years before. So I opened the hutch and dug through a stack of magazines I'd moved from house to house, until I found the picture I was remembering in my mind.

It was a gorgeous table canopied with white linens and draped with grape vines. Just lovely–candle light out under the stars. I'd always been drawn to that picture.

"Lord is that my table? Am I making this up?"

That's your table. Go get a Cinderella book.

This was beginning to feel like treasure hunt.

I went to my daughters room and picked the first Cinderella story book I saw. I went back down stairs, opened the book and was taken back to discover that inside the front cover in my very best little girl hand writing, I had written "Janet Ruth" long ago.

This had been my favorite Cinderella book as a child, but I'd forgotten about it.

I flipped through the book wondering what the Lord had for me there, and as I came to the last page I saw it. Cinderella and the prince were sitting across from each other, holding hands under a white canopied table with candle light under the stars. The resemblance to the picture in the magazine was obvious.

Come be with Me like THAT!

Whoa. He definitely had my attention now.

"Lord, is there something in the Word You'd like me to show me?"

You see, I'd been asking the Lord some pretty big questions lately about my calling and my place.

"Who am I? What did you design me to be?" And everything I was sensing as His answer back was ridiculously huge.

"Don't you have something simple and respectable, Lord–something less scary and a whole lot more realistic?"

And He'd answer back with sentences like: I'm big enough and I'm small enough.

"Thanks! I know I should be comforted, but that's just scaring me!"

A few weeks before I had laid out a huge question before the Lord, asking Him if I was hearing Him right.

No, He wasn't asking me to be a missionary to Africa; He was asking me to take the message that God is a Lover who rescues and restores to His Bride.

But what that would mean for me scared the living day lights out of me. It was too big.

So I asked Him to send me a blue Cinderella dress to confirm it. Knowing that if He didn't send it, I'd be off the hook, but that if He did, then He was in it and I would go forward. So, that morning as I asked Him for something from

His Word He answered: *John 14. Do not be afraid.*

I opened to John 14 and read: "Do not let your hearts be troubled."

As I read the rest of the passage, God ministered so many things to my heart that morning. He had me flipping between John 14, Romans 10 and Deuteronomy 30 pulling out commentaries and concordances as He was trying to communicate to me that I could indeed hear Him. That His Word was not something mysterious and far away; it was nigh, close at hand. It was within me, on my lips and in my heart, because He is the Living Word, and He is within me.

It was a glorious time in the Word with Him at my new table and I could hardly pull myself away to get ready for work.

I arrived at the office, centered and happy in God. And as my boss arrived, she handed me a small gift. She had been away for a month and was thanking me for holding down the office in her absence.

While unwrapping it I remarked, "Oh! How sweet! A little silver box with a bow on top!" If you are familiar with Florence Littauer, you may remember her teaching on Eph. 4: 29 about how our words are like presents that we give each other. She calls these word gifts "little silver boxes with bows on top."

I chattered happily relating that teaching to my boss, and then, "Oh, my word!" Blue topaz and diamond earrings! They were lovely! No one except my husband had ever bought me fine jewelry before.

I almost started to cry as I heard the Lord say, *I believe you'll be needing earrings to match that dress you've asked for.*

Later that evening, I decided to go on-line and search for information about blue topaz gemstones. Diamond is my birthstone, but I didn't know topaz. As I was searching, I came to a site about Aaron's breastplate and noticed that topaz was the second stone representing Jacob's second son, Simeon. Curious, I looked up Simeon in Genesis 29 and discovered that his name means "hearing," or "the Lord heard me."

And then it hit me. The whole day came together. God was telling me that I had indeed heard Him right. His Word was nigh, it was within me as a "little silver box" gift to me.

He had given me earrings to wear on my ears of all things to remind me that I could hear Him and that I was hearing Him right. I wasn't making this up; He did indeed have a blue Cinderella dress for me and He was calling me to proclaim His message that He is a Lover who rescues and restores.

Eight months, and many more blue gifts later, God sent the blue dress–that's a wonderful story all its own. And while He doesn't give me fine jewelry and dresses every day and some days the battle is so thick it feels like I can't hear anything at all, it's been an incredible journey and continues to this day, as God draws me deeper into intimacy with Himself and reveals His heart and His plan for me.

Jan Finnamore

But I didn't always walk with God this way. In fact, seven years ago, if I had heard someone stand up in church and give a testimony like this, I would have thought they were nuts and probably would have told them so.

It had never dawned on me that conversational relationship with God was available not only to people in the Bible, but to me as well. I knew God had created us for relationship with Himself, but I didn't really know what that meant in practical terms, and I'd heard hundreds of sermons on finding the will of God, but I'd never heard anything like this.

My Christianity was about having the right answers, and being good "to make God happy." And since I'd grown up in a Christian home, gone to a Christian school my whole life and had always been actively involved in church I thought I had all the answers and met enough requirements to earn my Sunday School sticker.

I had asked Jesus into my heart at a young age, been baptized and even re-dedicated my life to Christ, and while I'm thankful for my Christian heritage, my heart was lost to God, to myself and to the Kingdom. It was buried in a dark ocean of sorrow, and even though I had a wonderful husband and two beautiful children whom I adored, I felt angry, frustrated, grasping and trapped on the inside. But I didn't know it.

I thought I was "fine . . . thank you very much," and I was totally irritated at anyone who might suggest otherwise.

I never will forget the day when an over the top sanguine lady came bouncing up to me at church. "I've just joined a lady's prayer group and we've each chosen one person to pray for during the next three months, and I chose you!!!!!! Do you have anything you'd like me to pray for you about?!?!!!!??"

Bounce, bounce, happy, happy, joy, joy!!! I was ticked. I mumbled something in order to make her go away, but I stewed over what I felt was her insinuation. I didn't need anyone to pray for me! She was a brand new Christian, who did she think she was?

I was fine.

Yeah right.

I was about as fine as a musician on the Titanic. And over those next three months I started to see glimpses of my wretched, lost self, my inability to truly be good from the inside out, but worst of all I couldn't get through a worship service without crying. I hadn't cried in several years and to be standing on the front row crying in front of the whole church week after week was rather embarrassing.

My heart was so hard back then, I didn't even cry during Titanic. I came out of the theatre ticked at the movie producers for what I labeled as "emotional manipulation of the public." But through that lady's prayers, God had begun to soften my heart.

During that same season, the small group I was attending decided to do a book study of *The Sacred Romance*. The group leader said he had a friend who had read it and it had changed his life. "Changed his life?" I thought to myself. "You mean like how Suze Orman's books on finances have changed my life? I doubt it."

And so week after week as our group read and discussed the book, I never touched it, but felt quite comfortable showing up to group and mocking what I thought it was about. After all, I'd been in Christianity all my life, I had all the answers, remember?

I was making my way through a different book. One much more relevant.

You see, my husband had recently announced that he wanted to become an ordained minister. This was such a terrible prospect to me, I wanted a divorce. I'd grown up in a minister's home. I knew the inside story of what that would mean for our family. I'd seen my parents go through one church split after another, and their rocky marriage had recently ended in divorce.

So, I think in some ways, I was saying to my husband, spare me the heartache of ministry, let's just go straight for the divorce. But I couldn't do it. I was in love with him, and I adored our children. I couldn't leave; this struggle threw me into hour long crying jags alone in my room and deep despair.

Finally, one day I got the brilliant idea that if I couldn't leave the family, then maybe I could bury myself in a career and be present, but otherwise unavailable. So, I went to the library and found a book about how to be a strong, Southern business woman. Now, I was more of a Northern, no nonsense kind of girl–drank my tea straight up without sugar, but I figured if my career was going to take off in the South I needed a little more of that Southern Nutrasweet.

Looking back now, I'd have to say it was a scary book. It had helpful suggestions on how to find life, like: "Reward yourself for all your hard work. Save ten dollars out of every paycheck, then go on a safari and sleep with the guide."

Scary. But that was my "bible" in those days . . . and I was miserable.

Although I didn't know it then, God was actively wooing me to Himself. One day as I reached for my Southern business book, I became very aware it was lying side by side with the unread book *The Sacred Romance*. It was almost as if God was giving me a choice of two paths. Knowing that I couldn't do the safari thing, I grabbed *The Sacred Romance* and from the very first chapters proceeded to bawl my way through it.

Like the authors, I too had grown up playing creekside in the woods. I remembered being seven and sitting in a ray of light shining through the trees and feeling so close to heaven. I knew God had been there in the woods wooing me. And as I made my way through the book I saw for the very first time, that God was not an angry Sunday School teacher demanding that I sit still and be good, that I didn't have to do things to please Him, because I already was a delight to Him.

He had created me to be The Beloved. His Beloved.

Somewhere in the midst of all this, Curt had written a song from Hosea 6. A phrase from it: *Come to us Lord, like a soaking rain...come to us Lord, restore our souls again...oh come! Oh come! Oh come! !* He said, as he wrote those words he envisioned a farmer standing in his field begging

God for rain. If it didn't rain, his family would starve that next winter.

It was a picture of desperation for God. Curt said it was a picture of how desperately we needed God too. I was struck by the image.

At that time we had just built a house which had stretched us to the limit financially. I'd taken the builders to court over some minuscule discrepancy, and I'd spent the last of our funds on grass seed for our 1.5 acre lot.

After dispersing the seed, we experienced a 40 day drought. I remember standing outside with the hose trying to rescue the seedlings feeling my own financial and spiritual desperation, weeping the words of this song before the Lord. *Come to me, Lord, like a soaking rain....oh come! Oh come! Oh Come!!*

And He did. And He has. And He does.

That was the start of a whole new journey for me into the heart and life of God. I was overwhelmed with a hunger and thirst for His Word, but it was fueled by a hunger and thirst for God Himself.

My journals are full of the ways he has met me intimately since then. To know His presence . . . to experience His care . . . His guidance in my life and walk and calling.

It's been an incredible thing!

And the birthing of *Captive Heart--Love's Story* and the vision He's given me for ministry is a huge part of all of that. About five years ago, I became burdened that my children would grow up knowing God intimately as well.

I started trying to explain their fairy tales to them, "See . . . God is like the prince in *Sleeping Beauty*. He wants to rescue you from Satan and awaken you to Himself and restore the beauty of the Kingdom."

Then I started trying to write stories myself that would capture it more completely. I also began searching for Christian stories that captured this as well. As I searched, my urgency grew.

I found little in mainstream Christianity that portrayed God as a Prince rescuing His Beloved. Disturbingly, Disney came the closest to speaking the true message of Christianity to their hearts. Even more alarming was the "sit still and be good" dogma and the "sin management" principles that prese

Artwork from *Captive Heart; Love's Story* by Jan Finnamore, illustrated by Mary-Lise Fajal

nted themselves as Christianity in their literature and Sunday School material.

And suddenly, I started to see how whole generations of Christians could be church goers as I was, bound by duty, but lost to God and His Kingdom with our hearts shipwrecked as lost treasure buried at sea.

I've never considered myself to be an author. When it comes to writing, I'm the least in the Kingdom. I didn't pay attention in grammar class. My senior high teacher wrote, "I'm sorry" on my spelling final exam.

I laughed. I was too busy dreaming to care. I doodled all over my textbook pages.

I've had many attempts and much failure. But I do know in spite of it all, God calls me a light bearer and is purposing me to lay a charge at the root of the religious spirit–at the entry level and shift the direction of the future generations with the beautiful view that God delights in us, loves us deeply, pursues us for intimacy . . . that He is indeed a Lover who rescues and restores.

Jan and Curt Finnamore

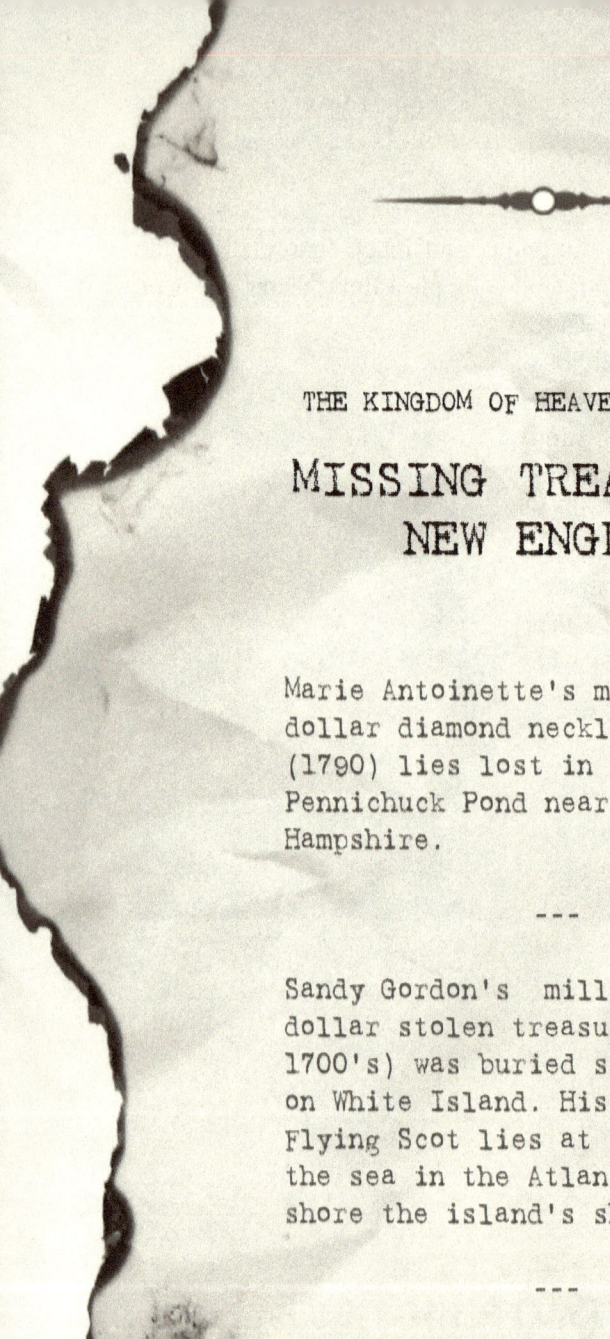

THE KINGDOM OF HEAVEN IS LIKE ...

MISSING TREASURE IN NEW ENGLAND

Marie Antoinette's multimillion
dollar diamond necklace
(1790) lies lost in the mud of
Pennichuck Pond near Nashua New
Hampshire.

Sandy Gordon's million-
dollar stolen treasure (early
1700's) was buried somewhere
on White Island. His ship, The
Flying Scot lies at the bottom of
the sea in the Atlantic just off
shore the island's shosre.

A solid silver statue of Madonna,
one of the most coveted artifacts
of the French Indian War was
stolen from Quebec and thrown
into the Israel River near the
town of Jefferson New Hampshire
and has never been recovered.
She is worth well over a million
dollars.

This Scene We're
Living in Is No Sitcom

We were born into a world at war. This scene we're living in is no sitcom; it's bloody battle. Haven't you noticed with what deadly accuracy the wound was given? Those blows you've taken— they were not random accidents at all. They hit dead center.

On and on it goes. The wound is too well aimed and far too consistent to be accidental. It was an attempt to take you out; to cripple or destroy your strength and get you out of the action. Do you know why there's been such an assault? The Enemy fears you. You are dangerous big-time. If you ever really got your heart back, lived from it with courage, you would be a huge problem to him. You would do a lot of damage . . . on the side of good. Remember how valiant and effective God has been in the history of the world? You are a stem of that victorious stalk.

Wild at Heart, 85–87
Daily Reading 342

FOUND: Treasure of Gail Cary

Heiress of the Kingdom

I am big enough.

*He heals the brokenhearted and
binds up their wounds.*

Psalm 147:3

FOUND:
TREASURE OF GAIL CARY

Delighting in the Love of the Father

by Gail Cary

I was born into a home that was physically, mentally, verbally and emotionally abusive at times, yet filled with love and laughter at others. My younger brother and I never knew if we would have the "normal" parents or the "dysfunctional" ones.

My father worked for an oil company while my mother sacrificed her nursing career to be an oil wife. There is a song titled, "I've Been Everywhere, Man." Because my dad worked for an oil company, we never knew when the next move would happen, just that it might be to a city or a town.

The worst move of all happened when my dad moved us to a smaller town, naively thinking we would escape the evils of the big city. Our big city mannerisms and the secrets we had to hide caused us to be shunned by our peers–except those who were rebels.

Drugs and alcohol were much more accessible, especially for me.

I had been sexually assaulted in eighth grade. The general reaction was that it was my fault for dressing in revealing clothing, but this was in the late 70's when tight was definitely cool.

When the pain became too much to bear, I could count on older people to get me alcohol or a joint to help ease the pain. My mother would take my brother and I to a United Church until someone would ask about the bruising, then we would change churches or not go for a while. God seemed like someone who didn't really care about us.

By the time I finished college, I was ready to take on the world.

I was engaged to be married, but broke it off because the relationship was abusive. I still remember my mom condemning me for breaking my engagement. She said I no longer had my virginity to offer and even in the 80's no decent man would want a second hand woman.

When I was twenty my parents claimed they found God. They said they were baptized; all their sins were washed away and they were starting new lives. My brother and I saw little change in their attitude toward each other or toward us.

I became very skeptical of Christianity, although at times I still prayed to God, especially during a hangover.

In 1992 I spent six months praying to God that my monthly HIV test would come back negative. It did, but the promises I made fell by the wayside. I continued to drink hard, and soon discovered that cocaine was even better than marijuana or hash for easing the hurts. I seemed to be living up to my mom's prophecy of "no decent man would ever want me."

In the fall of 1993 I chose to wind down the current relationship I was in and become a career woman. I also decided to give God a try. I was getting tired of hustling my body for drinks, pool games and jukebox songs. I was weary of almost getting hit when I'd smile sweetly and tell a man I could make my own way home after he had spent money on me in a bar.

At many times when I thought about turning my life around, I would sense an urging to move to a certain city. I always resisted, not wanting to move.

In the winter of 1993, I was introduced to a man from that exact same city. Six months later I did move; a year later we were married.

Life, though, seemed to be following in my mother's footsteps, with yelling, hurt feelings and some ugly moments that almost got out of control. In an attempt to bring peace, we moved from my husband's hometown back to my hometown. It did start to get better in 1997, when I joined my sister-in-law and became baptized–although I became a nagging wife always trying to make my husband go to church with me.

At first I didn't treat my baptism very seriously, especially after we moved back to my husband's hometown. But finally, after almost getting divorced, going through anger therapy, buying into the myth that having a baby can help a marriage and having a nervous breakdown, I realized that I couldn't do it alone, I needed God's help.

I stopped resisting the pull to the local community hall church and began going to a different church than my husband attended. After introducing my husband to my new friends, he began to realize that these people were a different sort of believer than the type my parents were. I was thrilled when my husband began to come to church with me.

Then one day he came home with a glow in his eyes and a book in his hand. A new men's group was starting centered on a book titled *Wild at Heart*, by John Eldredge.

As the study progressed, I noticed a change in my husband, as well as in the other men in the group. They seemed to have a more respectful attitude toward the women in the church, and they became manlier without being stereotypical male chauvinist pigs. After some gentle insistence from my husband, I began to read *Wild at Heart*. I got a third of the way through it and stopped. Jealousy rose up in me. I was envious there was not a similar book for women.

In August of 2005, I decided to take our three-year-old son and visit my parents without my husband. Although we had been married for ten years, my parents still seemed ill at ease around my husband. I felt if I visited them without him, I might get some answers. I prayed to God to guide me. He graciously answered my prayer when my mother declared in the car on the way to their home from the airport, that although they loved my husband, they didn't know how to treat me when he was around.

I soon found out what that meant.

The abuse hadn't stopped with their baptism. They had become better at hiding it.

Toward the end of the visit, I found out that even the physical abuse had resumed. In my eyes even a few incidents were far too many. Upon my return, I enlisted the help of a fellow Christian I knew in law enforcement. My parent's response proved that in many cases of spousal abuse, the couple will unite and attack the helper. I had to make the heart wrenching decision to let them go and leave them in God's hands.

Around this time, my husband began to share with me many passages from various Ransomed Heart books, although I constantly resisted reading the books themselves.

In February of 2006, we changed churches, in order to go to a larger church that had a thriving woman's ministry and a well-organized Sunday school. In May he discovered John Eldredge would be bringing a *Wild at Heart* team to our church in June.

I had mixed emotions. I was overjoyed that he would get to meet the man who seemed to be such a powerful Christian, but I was still jealous that there was nothing for women. The first night of the conference, my husband came home with a book for me titled *Captivating*. I asked if there was a journal to go with the book. The next night he brought home the *Captivating Guided Journal* and the *Captivating Live CDs*. He also told me of the Ransomed Heart Forum online.

I can honestly say that from the first page of Captivating, and from the first message I read on the Ransomed Heart Forum, life as I knew it ceased to exist, and I felt like I was embarking on a wondrous journey that would allow me to become the woman of destiny I felt was lying dormant within.

When my husband told me there would be a *Captivating* Retreat in September, we put the matter in God's hands as to whether I could afford to go or not. It was with both joy and terror I read the acceptance e-mail.

From June to September, *Captivating* caused me to go through many emotions: rage, sorrow, joy, hope, and contentment. It caused grieving for lost relationships and courage to create new. It made me realize that since reading *Wild at Heart*, my husband wanted a Beauty to rescue, but I was blocking that. I realized the reason why God wanted me to go to Crooked Creek Ranch was to help with the trust issues I had with other women.

Since September I have reached out to friends in situations that I would have pulled away from only months earlier. I have faced the reality I may never have the relationship I desire with my parents, but God has healed the many wounds from childhood to create a heart that will embrace other family members. Each morning when I go downstairs to my desk to read the Proverbs of the Day and journal, I feel God's loving arms around me. There are notes about possible books to write. The wounds are healing and I am learning to live a life of freedom, of strength and graciousness.

My husband and I recently embarked on a great

adventure. We took on the "wilderness" and converted our yard from something out of a redneck comedian's anecdote into something respectable.

When I read the Proverbs of the Day, God often prompts me to write out a verse for myself and for my husband. At times I feel like a beloved daughter, at times rebuked. Compared to the rebuking I got from my earthly father, the ones I get from my Heavenly Father come from a place of love.

I am experiencing a new world through the eyes of my son whom I used to hold back from. Now I completely embrace motherhood, confident I can rise above my past and create a new, better today.

I am a realist knowing that there are times when the Enemy will attack. I no longer retreat but swallow my pride and reach out, whether it is through church or by going online to my community of friends on the Forum.

In 2008 I will be turning forty. I know God will make my fifth decade a beautiful one full of precious memories. I am looking forward to the wonderful adventures He has planned for me, my husband, and our son.

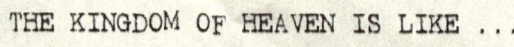

A COSTLY DIAMOND
IN THE MUCK

The ring was well-stained, and quite
dirty from its journey through the
sewer pipes. Yet something in its
sparkle caught Tobar's eye that
day in July 2004.

Knowing that it must have value,
he slipped the ring into his
pocket and continued cleaning the
drains of Nigel Shores, wondering
if the ring had once been a love
gift and what might have happened
to cause it to now be a diamond in
the muck.

Two years later, the South Coast
Water District of Orange County
is still asking that question: *Who
owned the ring?*

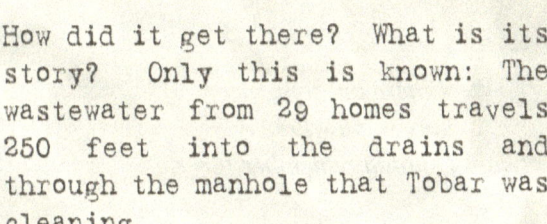

How did it get there? What is its story? Only this is known: The wastewater from 29 homes travels 250 feet into the drains and through the manhole that Tobar was cleaning.

Someone, somewhere, flushed the ring down the toilet.

Though letters have been sent and every home has been contacted, the ring is still lost to its owner. No one has claimed the 3.78-carat ring, and it's now up for auction.

The combined, engagement/wedding ring, has 10 round-cut diamonds with its center stone at 2.28 carats. It is near perfect. Its value? $26,000.

The Orange County Register

Were there but some deep,
holy spell, whereby
Always I should remember thee . . .

Lord, see thou to it,
take thou remembrance's load:

Only when I bethink me can I cry;
Remember thou, and prick me with love's goad.

When I can no more stir my soul to move,
And life is but the ashes of a fire;
When I can but remember that my heart
Once used to live and love, long and aspire—

Oh, be thou then the first, the one thou art;
Be thou the calling, before all answering love,
And in me wake hope, fear, boundless desire.

(Diary of an Old Soul)
George MacDonald

FOUND: Treasure of Chris Garvin

Valiant Knight

Come and take your place.

The final burden of remembrance does not rest on us;
if it did, we should all despair. Jesus is called the "author and
perfecter of our faith" (Rom. 12:2). He is the One who put
the romance in our hearts and the One who first opened our
eyes to see that our deepest desire is fulfilled in him.
He started us on the journey, even though we may for long
seasons forget him, he does not forget us.

I am always with you; you hold me by my right hand.
You guide me with your counsel, and afterward you will take
me into glory . . . My flesh and my heart may fail, but God
is the strength of my heart and my portion forever.

Ps. 73:23–24, 26
The Sacred Romance, 208–9

FOUND:
TREASURE OF CHRIS GARVIN

My Hidden Hunger

by Chris Garvin

I think I've always been hungry; always discontented; always haunted by a sense that there must be something more. I remember, as a child, pointing an imaginary gun at a thunder-head towering tall against a bright blue sky. It had a shape that to a child's eyes, could easily have been that of a monster.

No sooner had I pulled the imaginary trigger, then the cloud-monster slowly began to "fall." It fell sideways until it was swallowed up by a bank of low-lying clouds. It was magic . . . and I believed.

Moments like that have been rare in my life. But, they come. Even now, I sometimes find myself in a place where the light filtering through the trees, the deepness of the grass, the emptiness of the air, and the endless depth of the forest, all compel me to declare that, in that moment, anything is possible. The perfection of the moment is the proof . . . I am a believer.

These mystical moment have been my lifesaver; my light in the darkness when all other lights had gone out. A spark of life was kept burning in my heart, kept alive and fanned by the wind of mystery into a flame that burned within my chest. Often, later in life, tears would come in the moment –tears that I could not explain. But I loved it, and I welcomed them, because they made me feel so alive.

I hadn't even read *Wild At Heart* when I was invited to come to Boot Camp. I had barely heard of John Eldredge and Ransomed Heart.

I was at a point in my life where I was feeling very desperate. I felt unable to cope with any aspect of life.

I was not making enough money to support my family. I was way behind schedule on a construction job I had contracted. Deadlines were coming up that I knew I could never meet. I was losing my wife emotionally and felt completely incapable of reaching her and winning her back.

I had no patience with my two little girls. I was saying "No" and "Stop that" much more than anything else. I just knew I was blowing it as a father. And, through it all, my relationship with God was basically non-existent.

I desperately needed to hear the Message of the Heart; to see my life in the context of the Greater-Story. I needed to realize I had a place in that

Chris Garvin

110

story; an important role to play in it. This message caused my heart to awaken, to grab hold of hope and purpose, and to fall in love with my Lord.

One of my favorite stories is the legend of King Arthur and the Knights of the Round Table. God spoke to me through a scene that played out in my head during our "alone" time one night at the retreat.

In it, I was standing by the round table, with all the knights seated around it. Jesus was standing (as King Arthur) at his place. How I wanted to be a part of such a company; to serve a king that I loved; to fight with them for a noble cause. The king looked at me as if he knew me and kindly spoke, *Take your seat.*

Feeling as if there must be some mistake, I replied, "There is only one empty chair, and I can see that the name written on it is "Lancelot."

He then looked through my eyes and into my heart. He spoke, *You are Lancelot. That is your true name. Come and take your place.*

I am beginning to understand that Boot Camp was not about teaching me a new truth, but rather about reaching the truth that was already written in my heart.

There is so much to say about where I have come from, my father wound and my transformation, but for now, I must share one more thing . . .

During our time alone Sunday morning, I asked God what He had to say to me. What I heard was, *This is my beloved son.*

Of course there was a part of me that longed to believe it was true. But the voices in my head were saying, "How dare you even think that? Those word were for Jesus. How could God be 'well pleased' with you?"

I was trying to come to terms with this, and was still somewhat bewildered, as we came back in for our final session.

At the end of the session John shared with us the words that God had given the team on behalf of the men. I am confident you know how I felt when John spoke the final words, "You are the beloved. You are the beloved son."

God is amazing. I have fallen in love with Him. I want to thank each member of the team for the role they played in opening my heart.

'Till we meet again.

Chris and his daughter, Hadassah Garvin

✤　✤　✤

God, show me how to live.

THE KINGDOM OF HEAVEN IS LIKE ...

STOLEN WEALTH
IN IDAHO

SALMON DAM - In 1888, a lone
bandit robbed the Jarbridge
stage coach. Although he escaped
with a strongbox of gold, he was
eventually overtaken by a posse
and killed. Many believe that
while on the run, the outlaw had
buried the strongbox in a large
flat mesa somewhere on the east
side of Brown's Bench. The gold
has yet to be found.

WALLACE-KELLOGG   -   Sometime
around the year 1900, a bank was
robbed in the Wallace-Kellogg area
and the bandits made off with
some $80,000. Hiding out from
the authorities overnight, they

were said to have buried their
cache somewhere in the four-mile
stretch between Huettner and Post
Falls. However, with the posse on
their tails, they were captured
the next morning. The authorities
could not find the stolen loot
and presumably the bandits were
hanged. To this day, it has never
been recovered.

PRIEST LAKE - Prospector Zak
Stoneman was headed to cash in
three burro loads of gold when
his mules ate poisonous weeds
and died. Having no way to now
transport the treasure, Zak buried
the gold in the area north of the
Priest River and continued his
journey on foot. However, when
he returned, he had hidden the
gold so well even he couldn't
find it. Over one hundred years
later, those three burro loads of
gold lie lost somewhere along that
river.

IDAHO COUNTY - About five miles southwest of White Bird, lies Robber's Gulch, where nearly a century ago, a band of outlaws held up a freight wagon carrying over $75,000 of miner's gold and hid it among the rocks before heading toward the Seven Devils area. But the thieves did not live to return for their stolen cache. A posse caught up with them in the mountains and shot every last one of them before anyone thought to ask about the whereabouts of the stolen loot. To date, the miner's gold has never been found.

WALLACE - Butch Cassidy and his outlas gang allegedly buried some of their loot north of the old stage road between Spokane Falls, Washington, and Wallace, Idaho . The cache was said to have bee buried along a creek on the wedge of a beaver dam.

❦ ❦ ❦

FOUND: Treasure of Lady Rebekah

A Peasant Princess, Born for the Dance

May I have this dance?

I'll let you in on the sweet old truths,
  Stories we heard from our fathers,
counsel we learned at our mother's knee.
  We're not keeping this to ourselves,
we're passing it along to the next generation—
  God's fame and fortune,
  the marvelous things he has done.

  He planted a witness in Jacob,
    set his Word firmly in Israel,
  Then commanded our parents
    to teach it to their children
  So the next generation would know,
    and all the generations to come . . .

— Psalms 78:3-4 —

FOUND:
TREASURE OF LADY REBEKAH

A Peasant Princess, Born for the Dance

by Rebekah Garvin

On a Sunday evening in October, 2003, I climbed into our black '78 Chevy and drove away from the airport. Chris sat in the passenger's side of the cab in a posture that said he was present and glad to be right where he was. That night, the freeway lights came in and out of our rig as we made the fifty minute drive home. Normally, it would have been a fairly silent drive through the city and out into the next town.

But not this time.

Chris couldn't stop talking. He had too much to say–he was nearly exploding. I believe it was the first time in all my encounters with Chris that he dominated the conversation and really offered something from deep down inside himself to.

"Who are you?" I asked him, thinking I'd picked up the wrong guy. He looked like Chris, but the man sitting next to me just couldn't be my husband of five years and friend of seventeen years! This guy was alive and had something in his eyes that I'd never seen before. His presence held some new strength. On top of that, he was excited about something that *had to do with God.*

I kept looking at him. I could hear what was coming out of his mouth, but I dared not believe that what I was hearing was coming from him! It was literally too good to be true. It was like the boy I had known for so long, was gasping – sucking in air for the first time in his life and couldn't get enough.

Chris had just spent four days in Colorado. Little did we know at the time, but that trip saved his life and saved our marriage . . .

OUR SINGLE LIVES

If you'd have asked me what Chris was like before his trip to Colorado I would have said he was afraid to live, afraid to love, and he didn't know how to do either. He didn't have a clue how to be a man or how to take care of a woman.

Chris had dropped out of college early and ended up working as a framer in Portland. He had roommates off and on, but basically lived in one-room apartments with a mattress on the floor and a TV set; terrified that he would die in the corner of his apartment and no one would ever know.

Being alone terrified me, but I responded to it differently. Instead of withdrawing, I offered my heart to almost anyone–hoping someone would love me and fill the loneliness.

During my twenties, I passed through a powerful stretch of time that consisted of the loss of my soul-mate, three broken engagements, two planned weddings that came to a screeching halt, and a slew of men, colleges, cities, and jobs in between. I was the 'other' woman a few times and also ended a few relationships on the hunch that I would not make a good step-mom. There was abuse of every form. I lost my innocence to a date rape, gained an STD, and I was totally lucky that I made it through alive and without a child.

Chris' twenties were so self-controlled that it left him

little room to live from his heart. The quiet pain he endured was corrosive to his essence. On the flip side, I exited that time with a shattered heart. Some of it I brought on myself–some of it was not my idea at all.

No matter who's fault it was, what we went through as singles was neither of our heart's desire. I didn't realize it then, but my heart's desire for love and family had been under attack by Evil since the day I was born.

I thought God needed something from me that I wasn't doing, and when I did it, He would send the man. And until then, God's will was for me to be alone. I guess somehow in singleness I'd learn how to be a good partner. I'm not sure that worked so well for Chris. I didn't know the Enemy's tactics back then and neither did Chris.

THE EDGE OF THE KNIFE

Evil had Chris dying alone in a corner of his apartment without hope of any kind. At the same time, Evil had me dying alone while walking the fine line of being vulnerable as I tried to find that elusive "prince." The edge of my knife was flanked between two possible reactions to the pain: kill my heart or allow what I sought to own me. I could have shut down or I could have been completely destroyed by what I opened myself up to. Danger was on either side. Now I see that it was actually Satan who was working hard to destroy me–not God keeping something from me until I got it together.

Chris and I were both reacting to the World at War in our own broken way not seeing that Evil was taking us both out.

One of the biggest problems was that neither Chris nor I knew God's intentions toward us.

Religion and my parents brokenness twisted and darkened my understanding of God's heart towards me and allowed Evil to creep in among the shadows. But while God was Haunting me–drawing me back into the reality of His heart–the shame that Darkness added to my quest only served to sharpen the knife edge.

My parents accused me of not living up to the way they had raised me and made it clear that I was an embarrassment to them. They saw my adult choices as a direct reflection on them. But no matter how much shame and guilt they laid on me, I knew that if I chose any path other than the edge of that knife I would die inside. I knew that if The Prince came for me after I buried my heart's desire, it would be too late. I didn't want to miss out. Living and responding to desire was my way of staying alive and it did the trick.

IN PURSUIT OF THE FAIRY TALE

My quest? The fairy tale. Not such a bad quest. Yet true love seemed to evade me at every turn. It wasn't because I wouldn't agree with God and marry someone I didn't love and settle down in the suburbs. It was beause I didn't know the Enemy's tactics back then.

Naively, I entered relationships with men who I thought would turn out to be the *one*. Instead they would end up agreeing with Satan and laying waste to my self-worth. I didn't know what good men looked like and I didn't know how to bolt away from bad men. Putting core feminine desires in the hands of men un-surrendered to God is a dangerous thing. I had searched in all the wrong places, with all the right intentions, for the answer to my question, and got deeply hurt in the process.

Yet, I lived by the seat of my pants – willing to risk, hoping that love existed this time even if there were heavy consequences. Wisdom did not come easily to me and I had no clue how this princess of the Kingdom was to be treated. I knew my own heart was good. I knew my own intentions were not bad or evil. I had an inkling of who I was; I just didn't know how to love myself while in pursuit of the fairy tale.

There were a million-and-one ways for the single Christian woman to approach this quest, all of which started with the word *"wait."* Have you ever tried to tell your heart to *"wait?"* It just doesn't work. Not really. I tried to *"wait."* I tried to be "wise" and put my desire on hold. But there was really nothing I could do to stop my heart from being driven toward my longing for marriage and a family. That desire was so strong that it over-shadowed everything I did. I spent a fortune going to a private college in hopes of running in to my Adam there and discovered that men who claimed religion were some of the worst out there.

I would listen to the nonsense that married people preached to single people and my heart just wouldn't accept their methods of dealing with singleness. How was I supposed to fall in love if I was *careful*? My heart wouldn't put the quest for life on hold to avoid a little pain. True love had to be out there somewhere – and my heart was going to find it no matter what. So, I risked – in hopes.

I did make some childhood agreements with Evil about being abandoned, and he did keep me entrapped in cycles of destruction and addiction as an adult. But I did not succumb to the Evil that hunted me through the wounds of my father and

through broken men. Neither did it work when Darkness tried to eradicate me outright and then offered me the option of ending my hell by killing myself.

I believe the best way to take out a woman is to take out the man. Get him to wound her deeply and then maybe she will choose death of some sort and lose that God-given ability to offer life.

Rebekah Garvin

RESIGNATION

But the truth is, ten years of intense relationship rollercoasters took their toll on me and I finally became too tired to care about Cinderella and my dreams. By my late twenties I honestly thought that *something* would be better than *nothing*. My clock was ticking!! I knew I was tough enough to work through any relationship problem. And enough men had succumbed to my charms that I knew that if all else failed, I could rely on the intimate talent I had polished. My heart was pretty separate from that anyway. If I could just get someone to sign a piece of paper that said they were obligated to stick around, I thought I could work it out.

What I didn't want to accept at the time, was that 'relationship' really is something that is done *together*. The woman can't fix the man; it's not about her coming through for him. And sex doesn't solve much at all. Go figure!

GOD AND ME

In 1996 God escorted me through a pretty intense journey into a beautiful relationship with His Son. At the lowest point of my nightmare I found and fell in love with my Knight. *The One* rescued me. It became Jesus on whom I placed all my Adam expectations and I was okay if I was to be single the rest of my life for I had Jesus.

During that time, the search for the fairy tale began to look different on me. I was beginning to walk with *The One* into some wisdom. I was done allowing men to handle me and my heart badly. I dealt with all the memories as best I could and allowed Jesus to bring me flowers. I gained courage while Jesus lived with me and my doggie in my house on 'A' Street. He and I would sit on the beach for hours in each other's embrace (no joke) and watch the lights of the city turn on and the fading sun throwing unimaginable colors across the sky while the rhythm of the waves pounded on the shore.

I was *falling in love*. *The One* was an intense part of my life when Chris and I met again as adults. But though Chris respected my walk with God, he didn't understand at all. He had almost been driven to madness from loneliness and he was on the verge of claiming that there was no God at all.

I thought I could fix that with my story. I couldn't.

CHRIS AND I

By the time Chris and I started dating, it had been a long trek for me through the forests of men and love. Most of my fear was based in abandonment. Looking back over my options, Chris looked pretty good as he was as safe and as loyal as a family pet.

I loved Chris as a friend . . . had for twelve years. We met as children and had been best friends in college.

We had been raised in the same faith and we went through the same 'church system,' but there was a small rebel edge to him that intrigued me. I saw it even if he didn't. And I knew that Chris would not be capable of inflicting some of the horrible things on me that I had experienced from the hands of men.

He was cute and sweet. I'd had crushes on him and I had even offered him a kiss our Freshman year. I knew he would be a great roommate. He was far from flashy, but there was one quality he had that I knew would be of great value someday: He was a critical thinker. Not that his heart would always be in his well-thought out replies, but he had a way with words and he was always sincere. As far as bantering – it was not his forte, and the time he took to reply during even a simple exchange was extremely frustrating, but I thought that was tolerable. Little did I know how exhausting that would actually be later on.

On a ski holiday in 1997, Chris and I became a couple.

We had a romance of some-sort before we got married. It was laced with good times and bad. But though I did love Chris, I was *in love* with Jesus, The Great Romancer, Himself. At the end of all the devastating years of being hurt and used by men, *The One* was my Knight and no human man would ever be able to measure up.

I loved two men at the same time when I married Chris. I really didn't know what to do with that except that I entered into marriage relationship with Chris with few expectations – honest. No man could hold a candle to Jesus and I was done expecting them to do so. I needed a companion, but as for *love*, I believed I got what I needed from Jesus. My heart was full not because of how much Chris had come through for me, but because of how *The One* had come through for me. I actually had two wedding dresses the day of our wedding; one for Jesus, that I signed a song for Him in, and one for Chris.

THE DANCE

Back then, I believed I could glide through marriage by not expecting anything from Chris and just letting God love me. I now believe that *The One* can show up in a single woman's life in a Lover sort-of-way. And it is good–for a time. But when that same woman, who is dancing in the embrace of Jesus, begins to be pursued by a son of Adam, I believe *The One* graciously steps aside to allow the man to have his turn at dancing with her. By doing so, Jesus allows the man to reflect the Great Romancer Himself and walk in that glory. It's absolutely beautiful.

Since the woman has danced with the Best she now knows what it feels like to dance with a real (restored) man. So, when she accepts a dance with a son of Adam she will know if that man is reflecting God, or not, by how he holds her in his arms.

If her suitor allows *The One* to show him how to dance

with her, this son of Adam will end up reflecting the Dance Master Himself.

I was dancing with Jesus, but Chris was just watching from a chair on the other side of the room – never once cutting in on the dance and wanting me for his own. And somehow, though Jesus and I were very close, what Chris did *not* do was hurting me more than I knew.

MY HUSBANDS PRISON

Not long into marriage I found out that a safe roommate wasn't all my heart wanted. I wanted adventure and life. I wanted to be loved passionately, fought for, and rescued by this son of Adam. I had tried to get those needs met by men prior to marriage, but I just seemed to keep finding horrible men. My heart was breaking over the fact that Chris was sitting on the edge of the dance hall and not asking *The One* to show him how to dance with me.

So, marriage sure didn't solve my problems. Chris wasn't taking care of my core feminine desires any better then the men before marriage. In fact, marriage was worse, because I couldn't let myself find anyone else to meet my needs. Marriage became a prison for all my desires because I was at the mercy of Chris. And he had no clue what to do with himself, let alone me or my desires.

A LONELY MARRIAGE

I can not tell what impact the Message of the Heart had on *my* story without telling *our* story that lead up to the moment in the truck that October evening . . .

Three years into marriage, I remember sitting in the hallway outside my office suite talking on the phone to Holly. She and I were childhood friends and both of us had loved Chris at different times. Chris was a melancholy boy and he was mysterious to us. In college both she and I had tried to engage his heart with ours in hopes of finding a deep river of passion that we believed must be there somewhere. But with no luck.

Now, years later and all grown up, through tears I said, "Remember that deep river we thought we'd find in Chris? Well, after three years of marriage it ain't there! It really isn't. Nothing! I'm so lonely, I want to leave!"

But I kept hanging on. I couldn't imagine tearing two-year-old Maggie away from her daddy. I was strong. I could buck up. I was a survivor. I convinced myself that if I could just ignore my desires I could at least exist in the relationship and live on the memories of other loves. I might die inside, but it really didn't matter. I probably wouldn't find true love anyway – I had already spent most of my twenties looking for love in all the wrong places. I wasn't going to repeat that in my thirties.

So I survived for another two years.

During those years, our marriage probably looked pleasant to an onlooker. Though he looked like he had it together, Chris knew virtually nothing about relationship or caring for a feminine heart. I needed *his* strength – I didn't need him to lean on *my* strength. He was scared of dealing with my reactions, so he tip-toed around me. Bewildered, dazed, and confused, Chris was unable to engage with his family; he barked at the kids, and he barely noticed me. He often left the house with something remaining between us. His attitude affected the family more than he thought.

In his apathetic approach to life, he offered me nothing, or as little as possible, and hurt me with his silence. The relationship was lukewarm and was killing my heart. I had no idea what it was like to be rescued, taken care, of or fought for by a son of Adam.

I would go on as long as I could, but I had to engage with Chris, somehow. No matter how hard I tried, I just couldn't force my heart into apathy to. Sometimes my frustration would lead to a one-sided fight where he would basically cower in a corner and let me hurt him. I knew that Chris really didn't deserve the coldness I had gained toward men. But old feelings and pain would come flooding back into my heart making the moment much worse for me. I wanted him to stand up to me, fight with me, and fight for me. I wanted him to call me on my foolishness and be passionately engaged in loving me.

Unable to stand up to me, to life, or deal with non-perfect situations, he'd end up leaving or locking himself away after a fight to think about things all day and then come home sheepish and full of apologies and excuses – only to retreat back into his darkness a few weeks later. Then we'd start the whole process over again.

After five years, that routine got really old and the pattern was destroying us.

FUTILITY

Hating his job didn't help the situation. During the fifth year of our marriage he was trying his hand at starting his own company. But Chris isn't a natural entrepreneur and North Idaho winters can be brutal–working all day in the slop, sleet, snow, rain and bitter cold; doing something that he basically hated was not bringing his heart alive.

As he was dying out there, I was dying at home. Because he wasn't providing for the family, I had to. He left for work all day to make diddly-squat and hate his work only to leave me with the children and with the job of providing for the family.

I had a companion in Chris, but not a lover. I had someone to live with me, but not someone to add life to mine. I was alone in parenting. I was alone spiritually. I was alone in my business; alone in paying the bills. I was the bread-winner and alone in the domestic side of life.

Intimacy would wain for months. And when it did come, it didn't come from my heart and we both knew it. The *I love you's* were few and far between for both of us. I felt that he was hanging onto my apron strings and I was pulling him everywhere. I wasn't being rescued. I wasn't deeply loved. I wasn't even sure if he thought I was beautiful. And I sure as hell wasn't appreciated and wasn't being pursued.

He pursued my heart like he pursued life. "Well, it would be nice to be able to do that, but I just don't know how. I can't. It is simply impossible . . ." And so he'd tie his own hands and resign himself to not ever being able to have whatever it was that he wanted because it wasn't coming easily enough or someone told him he couldn't have it. He was giving all he had, yet it still wasn't good enough.

He felt the curse of futility but he didn't allow it to drive him to his knees because he didn't know who he would be on his knees before.

FATHERLESS

I believe Chris felt trapped in a life he just plain didn't know what to do with. He felt like he was drowning in a sea of *I don't know what to do's.*

It was like he grew up fatherless. And come to find out he pretty much did. His father's answer to his question was basically no response. Which might have been worse than the wrong answer.

The silence of his father and how it affected the thirty-five-year-old Chris became my worst enemy. He entered into relationship with me with very few life and relationship skills. And that made me angry.

He looked heavily to me to teach him what he should have learned in childhood. Where was his heart? He didn't have it, and it sure wasn't with me and the kids.

What we found out later is that the father wound is a serious one that is aimed at the heart of a young boy to take him out. And Chris was taken out. One can not give something that one does not own, and Chris owned very little of his heart.

A WILD YEAR PRIOR TO WILD AT HEART

During the summer of 2003 our church had a nasty split. I lost a big part of my life when the church split.

To add to that stress, in June we discovered that our youngest daughter, Hadassah, had Down Syndrome. It was the hardest thing I'd ever been through in my life. That summer I cried a river of tears processing my grief–alone. It was my worst nightmare and my friends were of little comfort. In their desire to help, they threw lies about God's heart my way that I had to keep battling–in the midst of my own heartbreak.

That summer on the Oregon coast, out on the deck of our beach house, Chris and I had a vicious fight. It was messy. It was a dangerous time. I would have left him had I had a separate vehicle. I just couldn't take anymore. Five years of marriage, a mortgage, two daughters, several life-threatening crises, and we still weren't one. I was locked in a lonely marriage and I felt I should at least get the 'single mom' title if I was living like one.

GAMBLING ON A HUNCH

Chris pulled it together enough so that I didn't leave during vacation, but his change of attitude didn't last for long. So, when we got home, I decided that I'd had enough. My heart couldn't take anymore. I needed to leave. It would be hard with two little ones, but I was a troubleshooter and could make it. No one had ever taken care of me before, so it would just be like I had lost a great roommate with favors who did dishes once-in-awhile.

Ultimately, I was gambling on the chance that I might get a reaction. I knew Chris cared and I knew he wanted things to be different. I hoped that Chris might decide to crash into my life and come close to me – either for a fight or for love. Deep down I didn't care which, I just wanted to feel something coming my way other than futility, apathy, or nothing. I had learned that the only way to get any movement within our relationship was through making him uncomfortable. There is value in being uncomfortable. And I was making him uncomfortable. It made him uncomfortable that I was miserable at home. And now I was ready to make him really uncomfortable by leaving and allowing him to rattle around in our house all alone. Maybe memories would haunt him and drive him to his knees for God and to his feet for me – or not. That was my gamble.

As I was preparing myself to leave – I had a date with destiny.

MY DATE WITH DESTINY

One Sabbath that summer I saw a video about some-sort-of Wild at Heart Boot Camp that was changing men's lives. A few of our friends had been to it. I inhaled about two minutes of the video and decided that Chris had to go to that *ASAP*! Boot camp? You bet! Get him out of his slumber! I always thought he should have joined the army to learn some life skills. Boot camp sounded good to me.

So, I got him into the lottery and he won a place in that October's Boot Camp. I bought him a plane ticket, came up with some spending money, and basically told him, as I handed him the tickets, "You either go to this, or I am leaving." It was my last ditch effort to see if this man would wake up or not.

The idea of four-hundred men on a 'retreat' together for four days and not knowing even one of them was terrifying for Chris! He'd much rather have stayed at home and watched TV. But he went anyway in hopes of figuring things out and saving our marriage. Maybe in the process he'd find some happiness. Little did he know that God would actually show up and blow him away.

Chris left for Wild at Heart with the key ingredient for transformation: he was *hungry* for something that he didn't have. He may not have known what that was, but he did know that he didn't want to lose his family.

Through Eldredge's unique style of meetings, Chris' heart began to open for God to enter in powerful ways. The movie clips and trailers spoke right to his heart, allowing God a point of access; allowing God to finally get through.

WAKING UP

Back in the Chevy truck, the neon lights began to fade away behind us and the oncoming cars threw light into the shadows of our truck. I listened to Chris tell his story with a tired heart. The freeway lights rhythmically floated over our faces as he described those past four days at Frontier Ranch in Colorado.

As the men were encouraged to do, Chris had turned his cell phone off for those four days and entered into a world that forced him to consider his life, his father, and the bigger picture. During the weekend I had no idea what was happening to him in Colorado–and I really didn't have time to care as I was busy taking care of the kids and had a speaking engagement that Sabbath at a women's retreat. To top it off, I was under some pretty heavy attack that weekend.

"It was like I came out of a coma holding onto a steering wheel going 225 mph!" he said as he leaned towards me in the cab. He went on about the father wound, God's voice, King Arthur and Lancelot, movie clips, world at war, vow of silence, his dad, his daughters and me, swords, Band of Brothers, etc . . . most of it was new lingo to me, but it resonated deeply within my heart.

There was so much that he wanted to say, and since it was a fairly quick drive home he was talking furiously to tell me what had happened to him. I was pretty much in shock and really wanted to meet this man called John Eldredge.

It was as if Chris was waking up from being dead; waking up from a bad dream. It was like he heard music and my voice for the first time. He was acting and talking like he had been blind and now he could see.

Those four days in Colorado at the Wild at Heart Boot Camp became the most pivotal four days of his life . . . and mine.

From his encounters with God that weekend he was now doing a 180 degree turn from the old Chris. And little did I know it at the time, but it would be irreversible change. Though I'd heard the word 'transformation' before in Christian circles, I didn't know such a thing really existed–not really.

Excited to show me what he had brought back with him, he pulled out a large bag from his carry-on and said, "As I was deciding what I wanted to buy there, I initially wanted to buy you something. But then I decided that the thing you want most is *me*. So I bought myself some books." He proceeded to show me the books *Waking the Dead, The Sacred Romance,* and *Journey of Desire.* I was shocked. He had never taken care of himself like this before. By taking care of himself he was taking care of me.

That glorious October evening, he literally didn't stop talking the whole way home and pretty much wanted to talk all night. This chatter coming from Chris was not the norm. This was normally a quiet, reserved, careful, not-knowing-how to-offer-himself-man.

Needless to say, that night I was stunned–but skeptical.

You see, I really thought that I would pick him up at the airport and he would say, with a forced smile and glassy blue eyes that that was the biggest waste of time and money.

But instead, he came back oh so different; transformed actually, and on the very first steps of a journey that would take him deeper into the heart of our incredible God and *The One's* intentions toward the human heart.

Rebekah and Chris Garvin, happy in 2004

I can't fully remember all that was spoken of that night, but I remember wondering if I was going to wake up Monday morning next to the man I had in the truck, or to my old husband. I really liked the man I was encountering and dreaded the moment he would leave.

I anticipated this retreat thing was only going to be a mild jostle in his life. He had experienced them before: a moment of clarity; a claimed change of heart. Oh, they were great during their glory and brought some relief to our family, but they lasted for about, oh, two to three weeks. The momentum of a marriage conference, a good sermon, a 'break-through,' or the application of a new-found trick, faded like the glow of a sunset. The heart still un-addressed, he would slip back again into depression, silence and quiet despair.

I was a little cool to his seeming change that night. I wasn't sure what to think of him. *I'll give this two weeks*, I told myself, *then we'll see if this is for real or if he is on drugs!* Although I knew he wouldn't be on drugs because Chris was a straight shooter – to his own demise actually. He never allowed himself to try living. He was too scared he'd make a mistake. So he opted for the safe route most of the time. But still, I was a little skeptical.

HEAVENLY MANTRAS

I truly believe that when God goes after the man and *if* He gets to free his heart–He almost has the women and children in the bag.

Could it be that Satan's mantra is: *Take out the man and that will destroy the woman and children.* And could it also be God's mantra: *Restore the man and rescue the woman and children!* So much hangs on the walk of the husband and father. It's true.

Chris' journey has so impacted my own that I can not tell my story without telling his. My walk has become more intense because of his walk with God. I'm even more in love with *The One* after Wild at Heart, because I've seen what the power of God can do to a life that hungers for freedom. And I love the clearer God picture I have encountered through this whole journey and the new cliche's I have to replace the old dead ones.

THE MORNING AFTER

After that amazing night with Chris in the truck, the next morning came. I so wanted the morning light to go away. I was afraid that the man I met last night wouldn't be there anymore.

And my deepest fear came true–or so I thought. It was starting out like a normal Monday morning. It was hell. It was our typical morning. Not enough time. Stressed out. The works. Chris was freaking out, as he most often did on weekday mornings, especially Monday mornings. Consumed with fret about his day, and completely overtaken by his own worries, he had often been unable to see the little ones needing his love and attention in the morning. Not to mention his wife's needs.

But then, as he moved through the living room in his normal tense manner, all of a sudden he stopped and said, "Whoa. Okay, I need to pray about this."

"You what?" I asked, as I stopped what I was doing and whirled around to look at him.

"Let's pray about the day. I'm feeling stressed out and I don't want to be, so I think we need to pray," he replied.

"OK," I said slowly, somewhat bewildered. He had never done this before. I had given up on family worship years before, and given up on him seeing the need to pray. I had totally given up on the idea of him joining me in spirituality at all. But at the retreat his eyes had become open to his mythic reality and he felt like something might be set against him.

He took my hand and led me over toward the wood stove. We had just started the fire and so it was still chilly in the house. He pulled me down to kneel. And with the kids running all over the house, he ignored them and focused on praying. He did something I've never seen him do before. He closed his eyes and was quiet for the longest time.

He began to enter the presence of God. It was like he actually knew who he was talking to and he wanted to talk to him!

Normally, when Chris was cornered into praying, his hands became sweaty and fidgety. He would rush through a formalized prayer – for he had no idea what to say to Someone that he didn't know and ultimately didn't trust.

But not this morning. He held my hands in his. They were calm and dry. Very unusual. He prayed for nearly ten minutes like it was the normal thing to do! He prayed for his day, he prayed for his girls, and then the clincher, he prayed for *me and my day!*

By the time he got there I was already bawling, yet trying so hard to keep my tears quiet so as not to interrupt his prayer. The moment was completely surreal to me, for it was what I always wanted: someone to come alongside of me and together seek God. He was doing just that this morning.

I was still crying when he finished and opened his eyes. He smiled at me, held my hands even tighter, and asked, "Too much, too soon?"

"No!" I laughed through the tears, "Bring it on, I've been waiting my whole life for this!" I sobbed even harder as he came close.

JOURNEY INTO FREEDOM

It was an unbelievable next few months. It was such a

Rebekah and Chris Garvin, in love 2006

drastic change and we both soaked it in.

We'd get baby sitters on the weekends just so we could go on walks together and talk about his experience at the retreat and what we were encountering in the books. Eldredge seemed to take what I knew deep down and put it into words. It resonated inside of me. I wondered if Eldredge knew me. Taking care of our hearts became a big deal.

Up to that point, church had been a big entity in our life. It boasted pretty big claims, but it wasn't freeing the human heart. We found out that the busyness the church had us involved in was damaging our relationship with God. So, as we chose to spend the Sabbath with the Trinity, our church life changed. Through that journey into freedom, we learned what the Sabbath was for and saved our energy for an Entity who deeply cares about the condition of our hearts.

On Sabbath, Chris would go out to talk and listen to God for hours and hours in the mountains. He would come back looking like he had been in the *presence of God*. He glowed. When he would come through the front door after those encounters with God I would rub my hands together and ask, "So, what did He say? What did He say?" And we would talk for hours. Then he would return the favor and give me some quiet time so I could go do the same thing.

Our friends tried to get us to come back to church, but we didn't want to give up our time with Jesus to go back to a place where God seemed to not be speaking. *The One* had called us out and leaving was a very big deal in our journey.

INHALING

Chris' experience has rocked our world. I saw a hunger in him that ignited my hunger. To this day, our favorite topics to talk about are the heart of God, our hearts, the War, our mythic reality, and our journeys.

Over the course of the last three years we have inhaled–

yet digested slowly every book, and almost every CD, that Ransomed Heart has come out with. Our God picture has become clearer through the Message of the Heart, as well as through our study of the Open View of God (Boyd). I went to a Ransomed Femininity Retreat (now Captivating) where I began a painful journey through my father wound and issues with my mother.

God has been walking us through some really tough stuff. We have journaled like crazy and have gained more freedom and clarity at the end of each one of those journeys.

RESTORATION

It has been amazing to watch my man come alive, realize that there was more freedom available for me and to feel the impact that Chris' transformation has had on our marriage and our family.

Chris now knows how to engage with his daughters. He knows how to love me. He knows how to offer himself. He's learning how to make friends. He is discovering his own heart and desires, and is beginning to act upon them.

A restored man is really a glorious thing. In Chris' presence I feel more like a woman all the time.

NOT MAGIC

It hasn't been an easy three years. Not at all. Two businesses have failed and we've eaten rice and beans for weeks at a time. There are still agreements to be broken and there are places of frustration and quietness. Evil has pounded us for pursing our heart and life; romantic dates are still few; and we are breaking new territory when it comes to parenting with the Message of the Heart in mind. We still hurt each other once-in-a-while and Chris has put a few more holes in the shop walls.

But that's life. That's life in relationship with another human heart in this World at War. The difference is that he sees his mythic reality and engages with me. He has his heart to offer me, and I to him. Whether fighting or loving, he doesn't disappear. Wisdom and revelation ultimately saves the day.

These things didn't come without being awakened first and then walking in the Four Streams. Thank-you, John!

What happened that weekend in Colorado wasn't magic. It didn't make everything instantly better. What it did do was jolt Chris awake and opened his blind eyes to see. And when he saw better, I saw better. *We* saw better. And *seeing* is half the battle.

OUR NEW REALITY

At the core there is something different about Chris. I see a man traveling with God. A man wanting to be whole-hearted. A man desiring to learn how to come for me. I never saw that before in him and I'd be a fool to not encourage that. Chris is learning how to dance with me and when we do step in sync it's breathtaking.

We might not have the money for Chris to lavish on me as he might want to, but Chris comes alongside of me now. He fights for me. He understands the burdens I bear. He walks with me through my own journeys and listens intently and shares the wisdom he has to offer.

He engages with our friends and he is trying to learn how to answer the question on our daughter's hearts. All the hearts in the family are important to him and he comes through for me in so many ways. (For example, currently he gets the girls ready in the morning for school so that I can pursue my dream of figure skating. That's a big task for daddy and I appreciate him so much for it.)

At my core I am peaceful even though the events in our

life have become harder. I'm done striving. I'm done trying to please. The home is a happier place. I do not feel the need to go into rants to try to get Chris to change. Our relationship looks so much different then it used to. I now know where to send Chris when he can't see straight. And it's not to my counseling couch. Into the presence of *The One* is where he needs to go. And I insist upon it.

BRIGHT FUTURE

Chris now wants to provide for his family by walking into the desires of his heart instead of gritting his teeth and doing something he hates. He's going back to school to become a counselor so he can help people walk in the Four Streams. He has started a four-year poetic journey that I'm so excited about.

This is Chris pursuing his heart for the first time. I want to see him walk in more of his glory. I want to see what that looks like on him. I want the world to see what I see in him. I want the world to know what saved our marriage and changed my life.

In our oneness we now have more skills in our arsenal thanks to the Ransomed Heart Ministries. We now know how important our hearts are and we know what is set against us and Who is *for* us.

A WITNESS

At the Wild at Heart Boot Camp, thirty-five-year-old Chris Garvin met God for the first time. There, in the mountains of Colorado – with a little nudging from John Eldredge – he entered the Trinity's presence and was transformed.

It has blown us away to realize that after a lifetime of "church" and growing up with the "truth" all around – available by the bucketfuls – Chris had never *really* met God.

Actually, religion was a place where Evil kept Chris dead.

Christianity makes a pretty large claim to change lives and transform hearts, but I literally had never seen it until Chris came home from Boot Camp that Sunday night in October of 2003. That's the night I encountered the Good News of Freedom that Jesus came to give. And that made me scratch my head, re-consider everything religious, and go in search of true Christianity – which has been a major journey.

God has been living with identity theft for centuries. His heart has been totally mis-construed. But His true heart towards us is unbelievably amazing and I'm am excited to say that I have been a witness to the rescue of a human heart first hand. The awakening of Chris has saved our marriage and opened up a whole new world for me – one that I never thought would be my lot. I have ended up with a very spiritual and authentic man – made to be a king.

On this side of Chris' transformation I can now recieve all the Biblical principles of loving each other as wisdom. I now know what they are for. Those principles of love Jesus talks about are how to treat a man who is surrendered to God and walking with Him into more freedom. Not for applying to men who were making agreements with Evil left and right. For by doing that, I was actually enabling the men I dated to be less than they were made to be. Those principles will help Chris and me keep the beautiful thing we now have. They were put there so that we can continue the love God has released our good hearts into.

I am called to live authentically and live in a way that reflects what *is* and allow my man to live with the results of his actions or non-actions. A flower that isn't watered – wilts. When I was finally done trying to paint pretty colors on the petals of my wilting flower to pretend all was well, and began to value myself as the royal princess I was, change occured.

Transformation didn't happen from a quick trip to a marriage conference or a quick trip to the local religious bar to get a quick fix tonic of tips and tricks. This was real. This was called coming into contact with the Warring Trinity. It was about getting Chris into the presence of *The One* so *He* could transform him.

My husband needed to hear from God about his life. My husband needed to know what he was made for. I'm here as a witness to tell the world that when a man comes alive to God and is awakened and transformed, a marriage can be all God dreamed it could be.

A WOMAN IN LOVE

So far, I've lived a pretty full and adventurous life: from cocktail waitressing to being a missionary in the jungles of Malaysia. But despite all of my adventures, this has got to be the most fulfilling adventure of my entire life.

I never would have thought it possible years ago, but our hearts are one. I now know what God meant by the two becoming one. Not one in duty, but one in spirit. That is Jesus and I. That is now Chris and I. Together we are a powerhouse. Oneness with my husband is the closest thing to heaven that I have ever known. And in that oneness I have found love. I am able to give love. It is now safe to be Rebekah. It's safe to be soft and feminine.

I am happy to announce that I have *fallen in love* with this man named Chris Garvin. And it is all because of his relationship with God. As he walks with God I watch him stand taller and stronger after each encounter with his Creator, and it is such a turn on!

Believe it or not, his personality is changing, and so are his looks. He is becoming more outgoing, and he is looking better and more comfortable in his skin. He is learning to love himself and he's becoming more handsome all the time. I told Chris the other day that I was now ready to marry him.

I can't tell you what it has done for my heart to 'see'

Chris and his brother, Jesus [or God the Father] walking along the beach talking about deep truths together. He walks tall and strong next to the Mighty Warrior Himself. He is His reflection. And that is so attractive.

Within this relationship I am free to be real and authentic. I am free to live openly. I am free to blossom. He is my perfect match. And I know that the more Chris walks with Jesus, the more my needs as a woman will be fulfilled – because Jesus knows me so intimately. He'll show Chris the way.

The *I love you's* between us come spontaneously from a deep place and we make love from a full heart. Making love to someone you are one with is incredible. Chris is captivated by me and I respond to him like a woman in love. And it is good. Very good. It has changed our life. It can be one of the lonliest places in marriage. Now, making love has become a frequent beautiful experience for us. And it is not from obligation, but from a deep longing to be close to this man who walks with God.

Deep down I think every man, walking in freedom, could be completely irresistible to the race of restored woman. Because at the core of a woman she is no feminist – she desires a real man. She dreams of being rescued by a knight. A knight of the High Trinity – a restored warrior and romancer at heart – a reflection of God and a son of Adam who knows who he is and who fights for her, a daughter of Eve, the crowning act of creation. By acknowledging her value as one who brings life to the universe, reflecting *The One*, he begins to rescue her. Wow!

PRISMATIC

A friend last summer told me that humans are much more prismatic than linear. That the human heart and the course of our life has many different facets as does a prism and God has healing available for every facet of that prism. Healing is available for the five-year-old and healing is available for the twenty-one-year old.

It's a good description of my life: prismatic. Only God knows all the facets of my walk on this planet, as He does all of ours. And He is walking me into each of those facets for healing – in His time.

When God shines His light on my heart – a prism in His Kingdom of Light – I want rainbows to dance all over the dark walls of this earth in beautiful reflection of hope restored.

HUNGER

My assurance is in the fact that now it's not duty that drives my husband, but ultimately desire. That river that I didn't think existed in Chris, does! It is a raging river of desire and passion. Desire for God and desire for me. That river was buried so far under all the volcanic ashes of Paradise that it took a lifetime of loneliness and pain to drive Chris mad enough to find the thirst he had for more life. His hunger compounded by futility and my movement was what eventually drove him to God.

He could have gone to that Wild at Heart Retreat and chosen not to respond to the Sacred Romancer. But he was desperate. He was hungry. And now I am flying over white water down his river that has become the ride of a life-time.

My life will never be the same again. My girls have a father. I have a husband, a best friend and a warrior at my back. And now I am a woman in love. Isn't it every man's desire to have their woman head-over heels in love with them? Doesn't every man dream of the woman who would think they are the bomb? On the other side of transformation it could be. I am living proof.

Born to love, born to fight,
born to wield a sword, born with thoughts and
words that transform the hidden into the
known. Your long sleep is over.
The terrain of winter has been your reality
but Summer has come to your heart.
Now passion and desire is what drives you.
Your heart is alive. You have found freedom and
are gaining more and more everyday.
Without you I would not be right.
You have been a huge part of my journey and you
have been the flame that has lit my fire numerous
times. Melt into me, knowing we are like hearts.
Lay your armor at the door of my beauty and
for a moment remember....

Rebekah to Chris - 2003

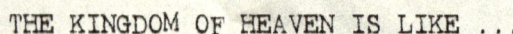

A MERCHANT LOOKING FOR PEARLS

*The kingdom of heaven
is like a merchant looking for
valuable pearls....*

-- Jesus (Matt. 13)

A mixture of helium and oxygen through electrolungs allows divers to follow the lime stone wall of Andros Island down as far as 400 feet. In pitch black darkness, divers search for rare shells and snails that collectors willingly pay well over $500 for.

FINDING TREASURE IN AN UNLIKELY PLACE

Once a woman moved into an apartment in New York City. She defrosted her new fridge and found a dozen thousand-dollar bills taped inside the freezer!

Oh, the treasures we could find in our own home!

Glorious Ruins

We are not what we were meant to be, and we know it . . . Abused, neglected, vandalized, fallen — we are still fearful and wonderful. We are, as one theologian put it, "glorious ruins." But unlike those grand monuments, we who are Christ's have been redeemed and are being renewed as Paul said, "day by day," restored in the love of God.

Could it be that we, all of us, the homecoming queens and quarterbacks and the passed over and picked on, really possess hidden greatness? Is there something in us worth fighting over? The fact that we don't see our own glory is part of the tragedy of the Fall; a sort of spiritual amnesia has taken all of us. Our souls were made to live in the Larger Story, but as G.K. Chesterton discovered, we have forgotten our part:

> *We have all read in scientific books, and indeed, in all romances, the story of the man who has forgotten his name. This man walks about the streets and can see and appreciate everything; only he cannot remember who he is. Well, every man is that man in the story. Every man has forgotten who he is . . . We are all under the same mental calamity; we have all forgotten our names. We have all forgotten what we really are.* (Orthodoxy)

The Sacred Romance, 93–95
From The Ransomed Heart Daily Reading
by John Eldredge, Reading 324

FOUND: Treasure of Katrin Jurdan

Restored Queen of Hearts

You are my restored one.

To all who mourn...he will give beauty for ashes, joy instead of mourning, praise instead of despair. For the LORD has planted them like strong and graceful oaks for his own glory.

Isaiah 61:3

FOUND:
TREASURE OF KATRIN JURDAN

Restored Queen of Hearts

by Katrin Jurdan

My name is Kat and I was in my fifties when my life was transformed in 2002. I had come to a place in my life where I was searching for more. I had somehow lost my dreams and purpose along the way. I had been a Christian for a long time, but there seemed to be something significant that was missing.

I have a wonderful husband and good marriage; we will be celebrating our 40th anniversary this year. I am blessed with a beautiful daughter and precious grandchildren. But my life with God seemed far away, and I felt lost.

I had been a Christian for over twenty-six years but I found myself empty, tired, and my dreams dashed.

I had been involved in full time ministry as a teacher and leader in Bible Study Fellowship and Community Bible Study for over twenty years. Then we moved to a new state where I became involved in a local church and continued leading workshops, Bible studies, and retreats. But there was still something missing. I felt so empty as if there was something I had left behind. I had.

It was my heart.

All those ministries didn't fill a void as I thought they would. For a time they gave me a lot of enjoyment and fulfillment, but I found out later that I was trying to work for God's love and acceptance.

I had lost my heart.

One day, I was wandering in a Bible bookstore having a conversation with God–although I didn't really expect Him to answer. I asked him, "Is there a book here You want me to pick up? I feel so empty and I'm not quite sure why."

I kept searching on the bookshelves but as quickly as I picked one up I placed it back after I thumbed through the pages.

Nothing. I felt so lost.

I started to leave, deciding that there was nothing here for me, but before I reached the door, a display table caught my eye. A small gift book grabbed my attention: *Dare to Desire.* Intrigued by the title, I picked it up and began to read the subtitle, "An invitation to fulfill your deepest dreams."

As I thumbed through the pages I found something else that struck a deep chord in my heart. "It's common for our journey to begin with a sense of discontent, or being lost." I knew what that felt like; my dreams had been placed in cold storage for years now and the feeling of loss had become my companion.

Then God spoke to me. (I didn't hear an audible voice but I knew He was speaking to me. I had realized then that He had not been silent, I just wasn't listening.)

You need to buy this book because it's all about you.

"Did I really hear that? Was that really You, Lord?"

It had to be God.

As I was purchasing the book, the sales girl told me more about the author, John Eldredge. She told me he had written several books, but the only other book she had left was *Journey of Desire*. So, I bought both books and left the store with a feeling of excitement and anticipation–a feeling I hadn't had for a long time.

I was eager to start reading and to find out what God had meant when He said the book was all about me. That day was to be the beginning of my journey toward a radical transformation.

Later that year as I led a small group of women through *Journey of Desire* God began to answer all of the questions that I had been wondering for so long. I knew God had a plan and a purpose for me at the very moment I accepted the Lord years earlier, but I didn't know how to get there anymore.

I had to walk into this story of God's in a new way. I had to let Him begin to walk me through my own story. He showed how much I was like the sea lion in *Journey of Desire*. I had been settling for a little mud hole when He wanted to give me the sea.

There was a significant verse of promise God had given me when my daughter was very young. Joel 2:25 "And I will restore to you the years that the locust hath eaten...."

I had been having such a hard time with my daughter and I didn't understand why. I was an abusive parent and my guilt and shame was destroying me. Then God gave me that verse and I held onto the hope of those words, but it was years later before I came to know their incredible impact.

I have a lengthy commute every day into town, so I use that time to listen to the CD's *Conversations with Ransomed Heart*. I remember thinking that the part about asking God for our name was rather hokey. But I would comply and I would pause and ask. I didn't hear anything but I kept asking every time John would get to that part.

One day I pulled the car over and asked again. This time I heard, *Restored*.

"What was that? What kind of name is that?" I

wondered.

I didn't think I heard right so I started the car back up and continued on to town. But every time John would talk about the name, I would ask God again. And every time I did, I would hear *Restored*.

"What kind of name is that? Couldn't you give me something like 'His Beauty' or 'Radiant One?' Why 'Restored?' I am so far away from being or even feeling restored."

But then I would hear louder, *You are my Restored One*.

Wow!! So, I claimed it, but it was really weird and hard at first to even share it. So, I didn't for a long time, and even when I did say it the first time in a *Waking the Dead* class I was leading, I kept my head down.

Slowly, my heart began to come alive as I embraced that name but there was much more to uncover, more layers, just like an onion, but I needed to be willing to allow God to begin stripping away those last layers that held the key to the transformation he knew I was ready for.

He wanted to perform radical surgery on my heart that would free me from a wound that was decades old. The wound of incest.

I devoured each and every book by John Eldredge except one. *Captivating*. I was bewildered by my reluctance in reading the book and this year God showed me why.

My grandmother (my dad's mom) had sexually abused me as a very young child. And even though I had a clear memory at seven of that abuse, I had blocked out all the memories earlier at two and three and then at four years.

Incest had stripped and devoured my essence as a very young girl and then as a woman. The image of God–that glory that I carried as a woman was devoured by Evil.

It explained why I hated women, and why I hated myself. Why I had such difficulty with my daughter, and

felt uneasy around other women. I preferred being with men.
I then realized why God had placed me in a ministry with
women for all those years. I realized the gift of my daughter.
I realized the full meaning of the verse in Joel and why God
named me "His Restored One." That's who he created me to
be! That's my role in His Kingdom; that's my design, and it's
who I am.

At the Captivating Retreat this September God showed
me my lack of forgiveness toward my grandmother and all the
agreements I had made with the enemy as a young child and
then as a grown woman.

I began to connect the dots of my past and began to
embrace the glorious image I carry as a woman for the first
time. Interestingly, it was soon to be my birthday and God was
giving me a glorious present.

After the session on the wound, Stasi invited those who
needed prayer to stay. I was so undone that day and I wanted
to escape. So, I was only going to sit for a few minutes until
I could compose myself and then leave. But my eyes locked
on a roommate of mine, and she hugged me and whispered in
my ear that I needed to stay.

The flood of tears began again. Another roommate
hugged me, and I lost it. I began to weep from a deep, dark
place. My weeping turned into wailing and then I felt this odd
pressure on my heart. I clutched my chest to try to relieve the
painful pressure.

I thought I was having a heart attack.

My roommate sat down with me and I could hear her
praying quietly. Then someone else came over to us and she
laid hands on me and prayed. Then still another person came
and all I could remember was seeing is her jeweled shoes.

The pressure began to leave but I was still clutching
my chest and my weeping turned into whimpering. I can't be
sure but I think the song playing was, *Resurrection*. And that
is exactly what God was doing; he was resurrecting a part of

my heart that had been dead.

My roommate walked with me to our room, and when we got inside there was my other roommate who had told me that I needed to stay.

I began to share my story with them about my grandmother and I showed them a copy of a picture God had used to begin this healing process.

They both listened and encouraged me to think about my grandmother and my need to forgive her. But I also needed to believe in my heart that it wasn't my fault. Oh, I knew that in my head, but that small innocent two-year old didn't believe it. I needed to convince her of the truth.

I needed to uncover the lies I had believed for all these years. They both kept asking me to repeat, "It wasn't my fault. It wasn't my fault." They kept telling me to say it repeatedly until I really believed it. I then realized that the intense pain and pressure I had experienced was the oppression God was lifting from my heart.

My roommates also encouraged me to write a letter to my grandmother. As I began to write on the back of that picture I had brought with me, I began to pour my heart out for the first time telling her what she had robbed me of–my innocence as a child and my unconditional love for my daughter. It had damaged intimacy with my husband. And it had damaged the

Katrin Jurdan

image of God and his glory I reflect as a woman.

I kept writing and writing and then I began to forgive her. I began to see that evil had taken over and that her own wound had ruled her actions.

I became sad that she died in her wounds without knowing God's rescue, restoration, and the release of her own oppression. I burned that letter at the bonfire that night, and as the flames consumed it and the smoke floated toward the heavens I knew I would begin to live differently.

The next day I felt alive.

My heart was at peace for the first time. That day's session was on the name and I didn't expect God to give me yet another name. (Since 2002 he had already given me several names besides *"His Restored One."*) The song *Royalty* was playing, and I heard God say that I was always his little princess and that he had been there even at that moment when evil had devoured my essence as a girl and as a woman. He was there weeping right beside me.

How sweet that moment was with God when he called me *His Little Princess.*

The next morning, I woke up early and I began to think about what had happened the day before and I began to think about this new name.

"You know God, it's my birthday in a few days and I'm going to be fifty-six. Aren't I too old for that name? It somehow doesn't fit me. It's sweet–don't get me wrong, and I love it but . . . "

Then I heard God say, *You went to bed last night as My Little Princess and awoke this morning as my Restored Queen of Hearts.*

"Did I hear you right?" I questioned.

His response was, *Look at your birthday quilt; it's written all over it.*

I had brought to the retreat a quilt someone had made

167

for me for my birthday, and there she was the Queen of Hearts. God used something tangible to seal my new name.

What evil had stolen from my heart, God now had fully redeemed and suddenly the meaning of Proverbs 4:23 came to life, "Above all else guard your heart for within flow the wellspring of life." This verse had become so much a part of my journey toward my restoration, and now for me I finally understood its full meaning.

I have found that God speaks more often than we realize. There is always something important about our journey, our story that He wants us to know. And if we are watchful and prayerful we will hear him through people, circumstances, heartache, grief, disappointment, loss, our past, and the list goes on and on.

He is always speaking, especially in our pain.

It's such a mystery how God can turn our life from something so dark and painful into something so stunning and usable for His Kingdom.

Chesterton says, " If you allow for mystery you can understand a lot of things, but if you insist on understanding everything you'll understand nothing."

❦ ❦ ❦

A FORTUNE LOST IN NEW YORK CITY HARBOR

In 1780, right off East 135th Street in New York City the Hussar went down in one of the world's busiest harbors. The contents of the ship included $2 million in silver and gold from England meant to pay British soldiers in America. Only the Hussar's anchor has been found. The fortune is still buried in 15 feet of soft ooze and trash and by now scattered along miles of the river.

THE KINGDOM OF HEAVEN IS LIKE ...

A TRAIN WRECK OF WEALTH IN OHIO

In 1876 a train traveling through Ohio pulunged into a river. The contencts of one car-holding $2 million in gold bars-has never been found.

THE KINGDOM OF HEAVEN IS LIKE ...

STOLEN LOOT IN OKLAHOMA

In 1870 Jesse James stole a million dollars in gold bars. He buried it near Lawton, Oklahoma. He marked the spot with a bucket and two ax heads, but was killed before he could go back for it. As far as we know the treasure is still there. Somewhere.

✤ ✤ ✤

FOUND: Treasure of Fred Pitzl

An Awakened Heart

Live. Awaken and be free.

Narrow is the road that leads to life,
and only a few find it.

Matt 7:14

FOUND:
TREASURE OF FRED PITZL

An Awakened Heart

by Fred Pitzl

Resonate. Awake. More aware. More in tune. Those are just a few of the words that describe my life since pursuing God more deeply through the Ransomed Heart message.

Yet these words don't capture the full story–there is something way deeper that words cannot describe. I have the sense that I am in the right place, that I can make a difference, that I don't have to be so afraid of myself.

Most of you who have read anything by John Eldredge know what I am saying. For those of you who haven't read the books, here is my story.

I was a faithful Christian. I went to church every week and joined the men's ministry–even went on a mission trip to Bulgaria.

I want to say I was living for God, but I was living more out of duty and obligation. It was the "wanting to do the right thing" type of living. On the outside I was the model Christian. However, I had a nagging sense of "there is something more," but I could not identify what the "more" was.

Then, by chance (or was this a divine set up?), a co-worker had a copy of *Wild at Heart* on her desk. She said her husband had just finished reading it and was deeply changed by it.

I borrowed it.

That was the best decision of the day.

When I got home I started into it and was jotting down all sorts of notes. Something connected.

Fred Pitzl

I got my own copy and read it again, this time underlining all that resonated with me. Then I learned that there were several other books—*The Sacred Romance*, *The Journey of Desire.* I even pre-ordered *Waking the Dead.*

Since then, I've read all of the books, and each one has brought me into a deeper awareness of who God created me to be.

Some of the many life transforming lessons I have learned on this journey are these:

My heart is good.

Proverbs 4:23 "Above all else, guard your heart, for it is the wellspring of life." I used to be taught that my heart is wicked and that I cannot trust it—cannot trust myself.

I was duty oriented and was trying to figure life out. I

have since learned that "life is not a problem to be solved, but an adventure to be lived." I have learned that there are no formulas with God. My heart does not respond to formulas, but to life.

So, I have become more aware of my heart, realizing that it's the "essence of my existence" (*Waking the Dead*). If I'm not present to my heart, I cannot be present to God. A silly yet profound example is when my kids wanted to get a trampoline. The safe side of me said, "No, it is dangerous." But my heart said, "Yes!"

I struggled with this decision for some time, and then responded from my heart. This trampoline has been a great family addition. I'm on it with the kids when it is sunny, when it rains, and even when it snows. Lying on it just watching the clouds is a great way to spend time with my kids.

So now, I'm more careful to guard my heart. Doing so impacts those closest to me.

Desire is good.

God created me to desire. "We sense a nagging within, a discontent, a hunger for something more." (*The Journey of Desire*).

This was a good description of my life right before I began reading the books. I wanted more. I knew there was more. I was being called to more. I knew there were spiritual undercurrents to this discontent. I knew there was more for me. God designed it this way.

One day I was making an on-line hotel reservation for a trip my family was going to take. My then eight-year young son, Josh was at the computer with me. He told me he wanted a hotel with a pool, a game room, free food, and wanted to be on the highest floor.

I just wanted a room with two beds.

It was then that I realized that God hardwired desire into

us. But too often, we stifle it. I have learned to let desire grow in me and have allowed it to shape me. I am now more aware of the desire behind the desire–why do I want what I am wanting? This has shaped me into a more complete person– one who is in touch with his desires.

Pleasure is good.

That almost seems sinful for a Christian to say. Desire good? It's more than good; it's necessary. Again, pleasure is something God has created us to experience. God wants us to enjoy life. He has to remind us through Jesus that abundant life is God's plan for us (John 10:10). It brings God pleasure when we experience pleasure.

A hike in the mountains, a long kiss from your wife, a swim in the ocean. God designed, provided this for us. I have experienced God's pleasure many times on hikes, on long bike rides, or just watching the sunset.

I am more aware of what God has created for me and how God has created me.

My wife and I went to Maui for our tenth wedding anniversary. Maui is full of God's pleasure–it is something He created for us.

We had the time of our life on that trip. It was our first trip away from the kids. On the first night, Carrie, my wife said, "Do you hear that?" I replied, "No, what are you hearing?" She answered, "Nothing, this is the first time we have had silence since having kids." Even in silence God provides pleasure for us.

We are at war.

To get the life God destined for me, I have to fight for it. I see more clearly that there is a battle to fight, that there is an enemy seeking to destroy me, take me out, to render me ineffective. "We are at war. The world in which we live is a combat zone, a violent clash of kingdoms." (*Waking the Dead*). This is the part most of us miss, or sadly, dismiss.

We do have an enemy and we are at war. A survivalist mindset will not take us far in a combat zone. We need to take on a warrior mindset.

Big difference.

If we want the life we were destined for, we have to fight for it. We are called to conquer, to put on armor, to be ready for battle. I now see the battle for what it is–a battle for my heart. We're destined for so much more yet we settle for a good parking place or a nice meal out once in a while.

Satan does all he can to keep us in this place of resignation. He'll remind us of our sin and convince us that we are worthless. The more sin focused we are, the less other focused we'll be. That's the enemy's strategy, to have us so concerned about ourselves that we aren't concerned about others.

I'm fighting a lot more these days. Fighting for my heart so I can bring life to others.

It is true; we must first be whole before we can be holy.

Fred Pitzl

As I journey, I am becoming a more complete person, more whole. I am a better husband, a better father, and a better leader. And the journey has just begun.

This is not a before and after story. This is something I am in the midst of, watching God mold me into the person I was created to be.

For it is God who works in you both to will
and to do of His good pleasure.

Philippians 2:13

✽ ✽ ✽

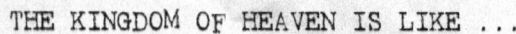

THE KINGDOM OF HEAVEN IS LIKE ...

BURIED TREASURE
IN KANSAS

MORLAND - While being attacked
by Indians, a party of gold miners
threw a chest of treasure into
the Soloman River near Morland,
Kansas. Overtime, the river
changed course and the chest was
never recovered.

Some sources claim that the
treasure, now under dry ground, is
a hoard of gold bars worth
$400,000.

ELLIS - In 1870 the Wells Fargo
office at Ellis was held at gun
point for its railroad payroll
of $22,000. According to local
legend, the money was hidden
just outside of town around the

limestone banks of Big Creek and never recovered.

RANDALL - In 1910, Davey Morris, a miserly farmer died alone on his farm about three miles south of Randall in Jewell County. He was known to be a frugal, hardworking farmer. For more than thirty years, he sold his produce for cash, and stashed it away in hideaways upon his property. After his death, it was discovered that Mr. Morris was a wealthy man, when various amounts were found hidden all over his cabin. Reportedly, Mr. Morris also stashed large sums outside of the cabin on other areas of his property, but to date have never been found.

❦ ❦ ❦

FOUND: Treasure of Tiffany Reynolds

Desire's Princess

I won't give up on you!

Arise, shine, for your light has come, and the glory of the LORD rises upon you. See, darkness covers the earth and thick darkness is over the peoples, but the LORD rises upon you and his glory appears over you.

Isaiah 60:1-2

FOUND:
TREASURE OF
TIFFANY REYNOLDS

Desire's Princess

by Tiffany Reynolds

I step through the door of my bedroom just in time to see my fatherless three-year old swinging her tiny feet in the air, clad in my glass slippers, saying,

"Mommy, aren't they pretty!"

I snuggle up beside her, and for just a moment nothing else matters, except that glass slippers are pretty.

I am awed at her free spirit, her delight in beautiful shoes, and her fearless, shameless desire to wear them even if they are too big.

I smile, remembering the day I bought them. It seemed silly really; usually I'm so practical. After all I don't even wear high heels, I wear hiking boots. But some how I was drawn, mesmerized by the sparkle and shine.

Well even if they had no practical purpose except to just sit on my shelf, they were on clearance, I reasoned, and if they were on my shelf I could look up at them every now and then and fantasize what it would be like to be shamelessly free, beautiful, valuable, waltzing safe in the arms of a good knight who loved me well.

I'm hit with the fact that I have settled for safe fantasies over real-life-big-picture dreams.

Once created beautifully in the image of God, made to live forever with a hope and a future, consciously caring for the earth, to be loving partners to each other and here I am alone, surviving, ashamed, holding my breath, afraid of God.

Here I am trying on fake glass slippers, pretending for only moments to be a princess, then knuckling back to the belief that my history and mistakes have made me never good enough, that dreams and loves will only break your heart, and dreading the day my children realize this same cold hard truth for themselves, or is it the lie.

I realize something is very twisted about this picture.

I look back to my daughter, still enamored with the glass slippers. She wouldn't have a problem with the whole princess thing.

Why do I?

If at some point as a child I was free like her, what happened, were did I lose it?

Where did I lose this beautiful freedom she has with slipping her feet right into these slippers, dancing, twirling around, being lovely.

As I think back, the memories fall into place like lost puzzle pieces. Dream shattering dark moments, memories reminding me of the moments that changed me, made me, scarred me.

Moments when simple trusting faith, personal value, and delightful dreams are shattered by the brutality, cruelty, and brokenness in this world.

We are dazed, hurt, scared and we re-adjust to make ourselves feel safer. We live more carefully, or carelessly, if you can call this living.

But one thing is for sure, we never again live so freely.

We spend the rest of our existence tiptoeing through the fragments of our sleeping dreams, trying not to wake them, less we get hurt and disappointed again.

We become survivors where we were meant to thrive, distrusting beggars instead of blessed, beloved, honorable children of the Creator . . .

My daughter's tugging pulls me back from my pondering.

"Mommy, it's your turn. Put them on, it's your turn to be the princess!"

Leaving it to my little child to lead me back to where I belong, I slip my feet into the glass slippers, tears running down my cheeks, the shoes fit perfectly.

I scoop up my daughter and we twirl around until we are so dizzy we can't stand. We fall back onto the bed and laugh. It feels good to laugh.

I have survived and now I will *Dare to Desire*, to breathe in deeply this life, to claim the hope, future, and place I was created for once again.

I will let my child show me how and we will make some new memories.

Tiffany Reynolds (Photo taken by Charlene Payton)

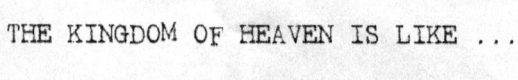

A CACHE OF
SPANISH GOLD

On July 30, 1715, Eleven ships
sailed off the coast of Florida
towards Spain. They were laiden
down with silver and gold to take
back home. A huge storm hit and
when ten of them went down they
took with them 1,000 men as well.
250 years later a man named Kip
Wagner was walking along a Florida
beach while he was waiting to go
back to work building his motel.
He was a builder by trade and
yet had a desire to find those
old silver coins that people said
could be found once in a while on
the beaches there.

That day, he was looking with a
metal detector and unearthed one

old silver coin with a date of 1715 on it! He kept going back to that beach, combing it finding more and more silver and gold coins. He gave the beach the nickname his "money beach."

Through extensive library and map searches he discovered that one of those eleven ships headed for Spain in 1715 had sunk within a few miles of his beach.

Kip made himself a surfboard with a glass bottom in it and one lucky day found the cannons and the anchor from the ship. Kip made a deal with the Florida government giving him permission to search for its treasure.

After a year, he had gathered a team of eight men and in January of 1961 while out on his first search-one of his team surfaced with a handful of coins and exclaimed, "They're down there by the bushel!"

They hauled up thousands of coins

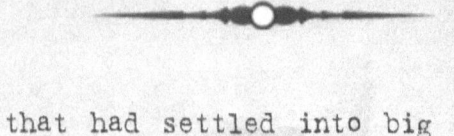

that had settled into big chunks
like rocks. That day they retrieved
$80,000 worth of treasure.

But that was only the beginning.
Their discoveries surprised the
world. They found a 10.5 foot gold
chain, a wooden treasure chest
that still was in one piece with
3,000 coins in it and 28 priceless
cups and saucers from China.

In his treasure hunting career Kip
found more than $3 million dollars
in treasure from those ships that
went down in 1715.

And this is the man who had spent
his life building motels and
thought he would never find even
one old spanish coin!

Taken from
True-Life Treasure Hunts
by Judy Donnelly

Heart – Not the Will

Though Scripture referred to the heart, I always viewed it in the way I do my spleen: though I am not really sure what it does, I assume it's important, wouldn't want to be without it, and I've gotten along pretty well without paying attention to it. What was central was my will.

Every problem could be solved if I wanted, really wanted, and chose to obey Scripture. All the commands and exhortations could be lived out, adhered to if I chose to obey Scripture. Knowing Scripture and choosing to obey it were central to living the Christian life.

I fear I was better at obedience than I was at loving God.

Craig McConnell
from <u>A Guidebook to Waking the Dead</u> (p. 46)

FOUND: Treasure of Tracey Black

Daughter of Royalty

You are so beautiful . . .

The LORD their God will save them on that day as a flock of his people. They will sparkle in his land like jewels in a crown. How attractive and beautiful they will be!

— Zechariah 9:16-17 —

FOUND:
TREASURE OF TRACEY BLACK

Daughter of Royalty

by Tracey Black

Me Now

Look at me now and you no longer see me.
Look at me now and you see the Son.
Look at Him and you now see me.
Look at my life and the words speak so fervently.
"I'm gone, I'm not here, and I'll never return!"
Become a slave is what I have done.
The life I now live is hidden and true life has begun.
Christ has become my life and I have
experienced transformation.
Daily I must crucify myself and listen to God's conversation.
Blindly is how I follow because I know His voice
He leads me to the path of His divine choice.

— Tracey Black —

I did not start out so surrendered to God.

I was simply a beautiful picture in a glass frame. A person could look upon that beautiful picture and see exactly what I wanted him or her to see, no dust, no flaws, no cracks.

I had it all together. I was a model child and honor roll student. I was involved in sports and student government. However, I was so wounded that I did not even realize the depth of my woundedness.

You see, I learned that I was rejected by my biological father even before I was born. He married another woman exactly 27 days before my birth. Growing up, I was a very withdrawn person emotionally, but no one could tell.

I protected my heart so much that the walls around it kept out everyone including the Heavenly Father. Nonetheless, I had no idea this was the case. I was a "good" Christian girl who put on Christ in baptism early in my childhood.

As a teenager, I had marvelous expectations of finding the man of my dreams–the man God wanted for me. When I finally met and married my "dream" man, our marriage hit "ground zero." Disaster struck, leaving me feeling alone, abandoned, ashamed, and disappointed.

On November 17, 2004, I prayed and asked God to send me a Christian sister who could be a source of help and support for me. Two weeks later, God sent Kimberly my way. His answer was clear, and I was drawn to Jesus.

Because of His answer, I knew in a deeper way that He was the true answer to all the issues of my life. This propelled me into the Word, and God saved me from myself.

You see, I had all the head knowledge of God, Jesus, and

the Holy Spirit, but it had not yet made the drop to my heart. My dear husband sought God with all his heart as well, and I thank God for that.

Yes, Jesus is indeed the "Lover of My Soul." With all my heart, I wanted to look like Him, act like Him, and reflect His image.

But it didn't stop there, not only did God send me one friend, He sent me an entire support group and the healing process began.

In January 2005, a dear friend from the group mentioned a book called *Captivating* that she was excited and impressed about.

I said to myself, "Oh that's nice." Yet, I never ventured to buy the book.

Then one month later, in February, God sent another woman after His own heart in my path, another Kimberli, and through her, He boldly reminded me to open my heart to Him. He was prompting me to be at His feet and journal those God moments.

Then another friend, Jennifer, told me about *Captivating*. Again I said, "Oh that's nice, I've heard of that before."

Yet, I still didn't purchase the book. Finally another woman invited me to join a study of the book. I finally said, "Okay, God, I'm listening to You this time."

At last I bought the book and took part in the study. It was an awesome experience. Then I learned of the retreat, and I realized that God was pointing me in that direction.

I signed up for the lottery, got accepted, and went in September 2006. The experience was phenomenal.

"Be still before the Lord and wait patiently for Him..."
Psalm 37:7

God gave me that Scripture after the first session of the retreat. I focused and opened my heart to receive what He had in store for me.

My prayer that night was a prayer of thanksgiving for providing an environment where I can be open to experience Him.

I so longed for Him to come into my heart, captivate me and take me to the next level in our walk together. That is exactly what the retreat did; God took me even closer to Him.

The desires of my heart became clear. Jesus touched and restored the tender places in my heart. I remember hearing the song, "Royalty." I cried so deeply.

I realized I had a father wound that went extremely deep. Although I had already gone through the counseling and grieving process of his absence in my upbringing, the place of abandonment was strong.

How could he marry someone else 27 days before I was born? Even after meeting him at age 17, we didn't form the close relationship I longed for. That grieved me; I desired to be reconciled with him. But I was rejected with a nonresponse. I felt abandonment, neglect. I felt unloved, unworthy, and ugly.

But at the retreat, God came for me. I went to the worship room, opened my Bible, put some anointing oil on my hand, prayed, and came back to my opened Bible. I sought to renounce the lies I had bought from the enemy. I asked God to help me know how He sees me, to show me how He sees me as a woman. I was so hurt at not being "daddy's little girl" and never ever having that opportunity again.

Tracey Black

Deep down inside I really did not believe that I was beautiful or that God would see me as beautiful. The first words I saw in my opened Bible were: "I will not leave you as orphans; I will come to you." John 14:18. Oh, this Scripture spoke volumes to my bleeding heart!

God revealed to me that He never left me.

I am "Daddy's little girl." My Daddy loves me so much; He sees me as beautiful. I know I forgave my biological father, but I still hurt deeply, until God came and healed me there.

Still to this day, He continues to speak to my heart through Scripture, through other women and through nature to remind me that I am beautiful. During that same code of silence period at the retreat, a woman I didn't even know motioned the word "Beautiful" in sign language and anointed me.

Later that day, I went to the worship room and made my way to the table where the Word lay open to, "You are beautiful, my darling..." Song of Songs 6:4.

However, I needed more assurance since I still felt unworthy and that He really wasn't referring to me as beautiful. I asked for more evidence.

In His faithfulness, He sent Jennifer to sing to me the words, "You are beautiful..." But she had been singing those three words all weekend, so I asked for more evidence beyond that. Then, He sent the snow. Simply breathtaking is the best description. I was so touched that I wrote in the snow: "Thank You God for Your amazing beauty."

"Be still before the Lord and wait patiently for Him..."
Psalm 37:7

The scripture continued to ring loudly and meant even more to me after the Captivating retreat.

Then the point of total transformation happened. I finally tore down the rest of the wall that was around my heart. God completely freed me from the bonds of the enemy. No longer will I live believing his lies.

I heard the voice of truth. My life is now a total life of worship. I am now a true worshipper as the scriptures says in John 8:32.

After coming back from the Captivating retreat, God gave me the name Sunshine, and He reaffirms Beautiful, Faith, and Sunshine regularly. Daily I pray and empty myself of self and allow God to fill me with His Spirit. My life is no longer mine to live. The direction of my life is determined by my Daddy.

The desires of my heart are passionate desires to be closer

and closer to my Daddy and Brother. He wants me to share with other women what it's like to live with a freed heart. Often He places a hurting or seeking woman in my path.

He has also provided women in my life who live with freed hearts. Together we watch Him work in our relationships to the praise of His glory.

The retreat served as the grand finale in my quest to choose Jesus and follow His footsteps of total surrender. I now truly believe that I am the Beauty in the Larger Story.

Thank you, dearest God as You captivate my heart and give me the passion to share my experience, strength, and hope with other Beauties.

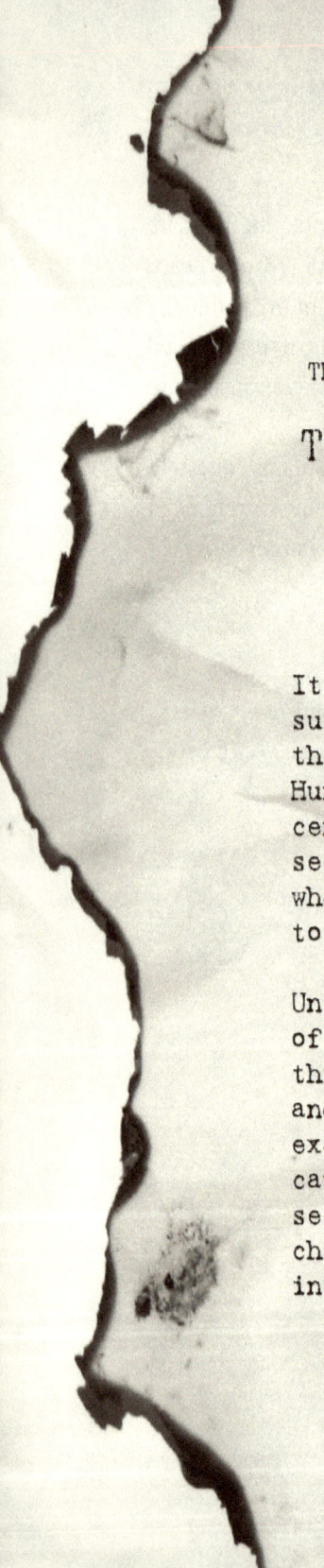

TREASURE DISCOVERED IN A FIELD

It was lying just below the surface, covered with only a thin layer of leaves and dirt. Hundreds had passed it by for centuries but never gave it a second glance...never saw it for what it really was...never came to know its worth.

Until one day, an ordinary sort of fellow taking a shortcut through a dormant field tripped, and now from his humbled position examined the thing that had caused him to fall. At first it seemed like a worthless piece of cheap trash, and he swore at the inconvenience of his throbbing

---

toe. But then, as he was about
to cast it aside, he stopped and
looked again, examining it more
closely. Could it be? No. No
one would leave a treasure this
valuable out here in the middle
of field for just anyone to
take! And then he realized: No
on knew it was there! ...Was
there more? Quickly, he pushed
aside more leaves and loosened
the surrounding dirt. What
lay before him was a treasure
cache of infinite worth! More!
Much, much more. How much was
here? He didn't know. What
he did know however, was that
the owner of the field owned it
all. Carefully, he covered the
treasure once again with soil
and leaves smoothing it all over
to appear as if nothing had been
disturbed. Then he ran home.

"Wife! Wife! We've got to sell
everything we own! I want to buy

---

a field!"

"You want to buy a field. Honey, we already have a field."

"I know. I know. But there is a certain field we have to buy. I can't explain, just trust me. Sell everything we own, all of your jewelry, your best dress, our house, our furniture, the kid's toys....everything!"

"Have you been drinking?"

The man met with much resistance as his family grudgingly obeyed. The neighbors thought he was insane to sell so much in exchange for field that wouldn't produce a crop. But the man dared not tell, lest his treasure be discovered. He didn't sleep, he didn't eat, the thought of owning the treasure consumed him, and the day he sold the jacket off

---

of his own back and finally had
enough to purchase the field was
the happiest day of his life.

❦ ❦ ❦

FOUND: Treasure of Gary Taylor

An Untamed Heart

Ride out with Me.

*But the godly will flourish...even in old age they
will still produce fruit; they will remain vital and green. They
will declare, "The LORD is just! He is my rock! There is
nothing but goodness in him!*

Ps. 92:12-15

FOUND:

TREASURE OF GARY TAYLOR

An Untamed Heart

by Gary Taylor

There was a lot behind my quiet smile when I was introduced as the "Wild Old Coot from Windmill Meadow Ranch."

As with many of us in our sixties, there was no way for me to unwrap for this small audience gathered at the ranch the adventures and misadventures of a life lived to the fullest. It was telling them of the life immediately ahead that saturated my effort to convey my determination to finish well.

My story is not one of fresh or even revolutionary discovery. By spirit, divine design and by training I was destined to be what my ego would claim as the "warrior class."

There had been glory and pain in the wake of battles over the forty years since graduation from a Christian college. The journey on the edge began as a lad of twenty-five with a $25M fire-breathing fighter flying off carriers and air combat over Vietnam and onward through a truly wild and full life of military, ministry, business and, eventually, ranching.

Gary Taylor

But I'd become weary, battle scarred and wanting something deeper, something more than skirmishes fought mostly in the name of Christ but mostly done without his full enabling.

It was way later that I found my center.

By the time I strapped on a glistening freshly sharpened sword as a Kingdom warrior, I was a grandfather, a retired Navy captain, a world traveled missionary and business entrepreneur.

I need to tell my story to give hope to "old" guys and to give permission for the young ones to set aside the popular distractions—the wound, the posing, the self-serving, the religious spirit—and become alive in heart and discover

Gary Taylor

your role as someone the Commander of the Angel Armies desperately needs for The Battle.

Being "wild" (read: multi-tracked with more failures than successes) was not an issue for this "old coot." No, it was getting God's permission to be unregulated, risk-taking and abandoned in following my heart after Him.

My discovery came in the usual unusual way and followed a life of "serving the Lord."

With the liability of being a loner, a weird one, someone considered strangely dangerous and a bit too zealous, I often did not feel truly centered in the Lord. So, it is the next, the wildest, the most fulfilling leg of my long life's journey that I want you to ponder.

But to get the full take on what there is about God's intervening hand worth noting, is to go below one more layer in what I learned in a nearly spent life posing

as the Great Adventurer—Godly, successful, a leader. Insecure, driven, and unpredictable.

Trying hard to be God's man–the story was still pretty much about me in one of those exciting lives of quiet desperation.

The drama began in an odd place. You see, mine was a life surrounded by beauty. There just was no person, animal or setting in my life that did not have the touch of uncommon beauty to it.

One could say it was merely God's way of offsetting my craggy, ornery puss and the well-worn, oft crusty, ranchers work outfit that typified my persona.

My wife, my son, my daughter and her children, the valley, the huge log ranch house and cabins, even the horses, dogs, and, yes, the barn cats all seemed striking as if cast in Hollywood.

I'd work hard to appear humble as if I had anything to do with this, but it was the signature touch of unearned grace. But that was about to change; not the grace, but the way this wonderfully irregular God was going to overlay his imprimatur on my life.

The new leg of my life journey began simply enough. I had elbowed a copy of *The Sacred Romance* over to Darick sitting at his desk next to mine in our ranch house office. (You don't suggest too loudly to your son of thirty-two years that he needs to be more spiritual or maybe could act a bit more like the son of a missionary businessman.)

Darick had un-enrolled the day his two-year wait for the Colorado Springs Police Academy was over. God said to him more clearly than He'd said anything directly to him, *Help your Mom and Dad save the business and save the ranch.*

We'd developed a global communications system that would enable tourists to make calls from public pay phone on credit cards. It was a boon to Americans unused to phone cards and seldom having the right "foreign" change in their pockets for the ever-present pay phones in Europe and Asia.

I was over my head in the very technology Darick's years in the Air Force made him a "whiz kid" at.

My business agents were typically daring young men willing to cross radical cultural barriers to deliver the Good News of Christ—missionaries—mostly to "closed" Muslim countries.

But these were guys who needed something other than a pith helmet and big Bible under their arm as a reason to be hanging around in the market suq.

Then Darick, the tech sergeant and would-be patrolman became a better captain of the ship than this real life captain, so he began to meet with our guys in some of the world's most interesting places . . . Turkey, Pakistan, Indonesia, Malaysia. He really liked "our guys" and showed he was touched by their insights in life and their dedication to their call.

Eventually, and I don't know when for sure, Darick read *The Sacred Romance.* But it was sometime in the fall of '99. Clearly, but slowly his life was changing.

For the first time in way too many years we were actually enjoying each other. Respect and humor returned. We were entering the Thanksgiving-to-Christmas family season with a new anticipation. It was coming time for the Christmas visit with my daughter, Cari, and her husband,

Matt, whom we all adored (or whatever cowboys do with men they really admire and enjoy) and, of course, their one and a half sons.

We never made the trip to Utah and the brother-sister reunion from years of separation. The drama that followed took four months, but it unfolded in what is still a blur.

On the trip out in a rented van as we were all traveling together to Cari's in Utah, Darick was overcome by a mysterious and extreme pain. The nearest mountain town with EMT services was a half hour away. They directed us to the hospital over the pass, another half hour. It took the excruciatingly long trip back to the big city to learn that those clouded lungs shown on the urgent care x-ray were not pneumonia. On Christmas Eve, we learned Darick was in fourth stage lung cancer.

He died four months later.

Life, we learned midst the successes, the beauty, the adventure, is short. It is hard, It is unfair. It's end is unpredictable. Dealing with it and dealing with the pain when "short, hard, unfair and unpredictable" comes due, mapped the first leg of a new adventure. That start is pegged around the "wild and amazing discoveries" Darick articulated in his closing days.

Keep this in mind: The transformation had begun early in the fall after pondering, discussing, and applying the "new" truths of a living romance with a personal God who deeply cares.

Millennium eve was one week after the discovery of Cancer. Prompted by a statement that humbled his high-profile Christian dad, Darick began a testimony as friends gathered around the flaming fireplace close to the midnight that would begin a new century and a new frame for viewing life by his small audience.

"This," referring to the life of grace, freedom, unscripted and deeply personal faith he'd discovered in a

Jesus who pursued him faithfully during "wayward" years, "was the Christianity I wish I could have known all my life."

"If you would ask if I'd trade what I know now of walking with God for this cancer, I would say, 'Hell no!' I hope I have a long life ahead to enjoy Him, but if I don't, I know what I have found is worth it."

If the Apostle's reference to his life profile as a race to be finished well, then I discovered I was being set up. It was grace amplified and redirected.

Leg two of the new journey began and now continues with "son" number two, the one married to Cari. When Matt lost his dad within two months of Darick's death, Matt and I discovered God had arranged for a swap, sort of like giving each of us a baton from the other team's stumbling teammate. "Pops," he would say. "Son," I would reply.

The discovery sharpened in Ransomed Heart's boot camp. It wasn't enough for this slow learner, so I was back for the advanced.

Proximity to RHM, the ranch and guest cabins and the horses played nicely to get up close and personal with the "youngins" of the RHM team and their families–cowpokes all.

Quickly Matt and I grew the sense of being on the front lines of warfare, a two-man band of brothers. How remarkable that two in-laws became best friends and comrades, separated by a generation, joined by strange providence.

Now comes the lesson of leg two which has become leg three, the longest of this journey that includes both of us. Paul, with one startling exception in Athens, was always with a partner or two in ministry.

David had Jonathan. Even the Lone Ranger had Tanto and I had always flown into combat with a wingman.

Most solo heroes, the Medal of Honor winners, are dead, most the rest are badly wounded; all noble, but finished. So, having learned only too well how the heroic world-missions, change-the-world crusade of the first sixty-years of my youth had left me "finished," hanging out in the wind, I embraced Matt, my comrade of heart and hand, deeply.

It's the long rides on horses and ORV's, almost always in the late night when wives and grandwonderkids (now four) are asleep, almost always in wild, dangerous and agreeably stupid adventures, but every time with a beer and a cigar that marks our private "R and R" from our daily foxhole experiences (Matt's a therapist for really screwed up kids at a residential treatment ranch).

Accountability? Yeah, for his addictions and mine. Comradeship, yeah, for the critical recognition that no warrior is without his band.

Fun? Uh-huh; what else would you call riding in total darkness through a forest and along canyon walls with no clue how we got lost or how to fix it.

Passion? You bet, for the unmatched sense of teaming up to nurture "our" four—three really tough mini-cowboys and a no-nonsense beauty of four years—to be the spear's head together for the good and godly warriors and captivating princesses of our next generations.

Thrilling? How else could you describe belonging to each other and to the Father until He walks us the final steps to His altar ending the sacred romance and beginning the eternal embrace with the Lover of our souls . . . and cherishing Darick who's been helping Jesus build a new ranch on a gorgeous overlook?

So, this old coot from Windmill Meadow Ranch is

Gary and Caroline Taylor

finishing well. It's not by accident and not by habit, but by choice . . . and not alone.

If I strapped on the full armor a bit late, the point of my story is the choice, not the timing. The choice was no longer to live out the compulsions of success but to trust my heart and his design in me to walk with God as His friend and warrior-companion.

❦ ❦ ❦

VICTORY OVER A VILLAIN

It is said that the mere sight of his ship weakened even the bravest captain. Edward Teach was a giant of a man. When preparing to attack, he would strap an assortment of loaded pistols across his chest. Daggers and a broad cutlass would hang at his side. Filled with slow burning match fuses and smoldering with flames, his braided hair and beard would stand wildly on end. Blackbeard, struck terror in the hearts of all who saw him.

Piracy was rampant in the early 1700's on the North American East Coast. There was no such thing as pleasure cruise. No one knew if their crop would arrive safely at port, if their loved ones would reach their destination unharmed...passengers, sailors and merchants alike lived in constant fear of being attacked, robbed, kidnapped or killed.

For years as Blackbeard roamed the East Coast and the Caribbean looking for something to steal...someone to kill...something to destroy, the terrorized colonists petitioned the officials to no avail. They'd been bought off. The Royal Governor, Charles Eden of North Carolina benefited handsomely from Blackbeard's exploits, and in fact, made the pirate feel so welcome in the colony that Blackbeard felt comfortable enough to build several opulent homes for his 13 wives.

At last, the colonists were able to convince Governor Spotswood of Virginia to send Lieutenant Robert Maynard and a ship of soldiers to capture or kill the

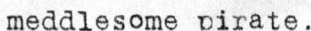

meddlesome pirate.

On November 22, 1718, Maynard
spotted Blackbeard's ship in
Ocracoke inlet. Cannons boomed.
War ensued. And as a cannonball
from Blackbeard's ship caused
the Virginia vessel to become
stranded on a sandbar, Blackbeard
raised his flag, lit his fuses
and boarded the weakened war
ship.

Soon Maynard and Blackbeard were
face to face, swords drawn. A
single slice from the pirate's
cutlass broke the Lieutenant's
sword in half. Now defenseless,
he could be easily run through.
But as the wild eyed pirate
raised his blade, a sailor from
behind swung with all his might.

Blackbeard's smoldering, grisly
head fell to the deck.

Upon winning the battle, Maynard
tied the pirate's head to the

---

bowsprit. Sailing homeward past
all of the villages and seaports,
all could see their villain was
conquered at last.

THE SONG

There is a melody that has haunted me my entire life.
I'm sure I first heard it in the womb in my mothers heartbeat,
and later in her voice as she held me and spoke my name.
But it wasn't my mother's song.

I'm sure I heard it in my father's laughter and in the
silly lullabies he would make up as he sang me off to sleep.
But it wasn't my father's song.

As a young boy I heard the song in my dreams,
calling to me from beyond sleep.
But the song did not belong to my dreams.

As a child the music began to come from beyond my mother
and father, from beyond me and beyond all that was familiar.
It would drift in through an open window
on the whisper of a breeze.
From the roof in the sound of pounding rain,
or through the distant sound of thunder.
All seemed to carry something with them that was more than
the sound of themselves.
For the song did not belong to them.

As a young man, the song seemed to be carried even
by things that had no sound of their own.
The sun setting over the ocean.
The sunrise in my rear view mirror.
The turning of leaves in the fall.
The first snow of winter on the mountains.
Even silence itself seemed to carry this tune –
sometimes louder than anything else.
But the tune did not belong to the silence.

As an adult, the music of the song came from everywhere,
often from many places at the same time.
From within my heart. From my memories.
From distant stars and from beyond the horizon.
From the beauty and the mystery of creation.
From the words of poems and stories.
But the music was not theirs.

I wondered where the song came from.

I began to suspect that all I had been hearing
were echoes of an ancient melody.
Just the faint haunting strains of The Song.
The Song which I had yet to hear in it's fullness.
The Song whose complete richness and beauty
I had yet to experience.

– Anonymous –
[used with permission]

❧ ❧ ❧

FOUND: Treasure of The One

The Longing of Mithril

I am coming for you.

A white-tailed deer drinks from the creek;
I want to drink God, deep draughts of God.
I'm thirsty for God-alive.

Psalms 42:1-2

Christianity has nothing to say to the person who is completely
happy with the way things are. Its message is for those who
hunger and thirst—for those who desire life as it
was meant to be.

The Journey of Desire, 43

FOUND:
TREASURE OF THE ONE

My Longing

by Mithril

There is a void in my soul that has vexed me all my life. I have known about it since I was a little girl, though unaware of its source. It has followed me wherever I go.

Whenever I sit still it comes up from my stomach and almost chokes me with the grief that it reveals. Sometimes I have tried to out run the presence of it. Other times I have tried to fill the aching with things, people or experiences I can find on this planet. Often I have tried to put words to the ache, to the deep void, with little luck. Sometimes I am able to ignore it for awhile.

But no matter what I do I have not been able to shake it off or run from it. Instead, it has become the very essence of me and I have begun to embrace the hunger that it creates within me as who I am.

The void has revealed itself in many ways. One way is the constant conflict between how I see my mythic reality and the reality we can all see. What is available in this life within the ashes of Paradise does not match what my heart sees, needs and knows it could be or have.

This conflict has lead to an unresolved longing that has expanded that void until I feel the very presence of the ache every moment of my awareness.

THE VOID REVEALED

This past decade's journey has revealed the shape and purpose of the void that seems to have almost taken over my being. I have stared into the vastness of its darkness and felt the unrelenting sadness that it seems to have tattooed on my heart. Living with its presence has forced it into every corner of my existence until it spilled out onto the porches of my life. So that now, at thirty-seven-years old, it is as deep within me as is my very core.

It is my core.

I can not be defined apart from it.

Contradictory as it may seem, it is as though this persistent and heavy darkness actually awakens the Immortal hope that abounds there in my heart. So I allow the presence to consume me. The hunger that is causes is the very life blood of my being.

To experience the restoration of the Light that once lived there is my purpose for living. It is the center of my desire. Walking within the truth the darkness reveals, this void as my journey's companion–for now–I hope to find a left-over remnant from an ancient time long ago.

A glorious ruin. A memory, a scent, an image of a love that I am destined to have once again.

So, I search out the corners of the darkness and I walk into the shadow of something that once was.

Truly something amazing existed there long ago. Something that stirred my heart and filled it to overflowing. Though I can not partake in the riches of that time–yet, still I am drawn to those shadows because I have had glimpses of the haunting reflection of what used to dwell there.

And it was breathtaking.

It is the absence of that reality and the un-fulfillment of that memory that has gripped my heart with a sadness that manifests itself as hunger and to which I owe the depth of the abyss I have felt in my heart since I was a young girl.

The good news is that I have seen the hope that lies in the darkness of that void.

There have been moments walking in the darkness when I have smelled a familiar smell. My head turns and I try to remember that scent. I want it to linger. But it goes as quickly as it came.

I have tasted a familiar taste and I only want more. It reminds me of something, but what is it? It tickles the corners of my mind. It haunts my heart. I've been here before. Dejavu at its best.

I've felt something wonderfully warm caress my skin and I have felt its desire for me. I've heard the music and I've twirled in its caress and for a moment we dance together, but the cold wind comes whistling through that tunnel all too fast and carries the music away with it.

Small flickers of light pierce the darkness and my eyes lock onto that point and I follow. But like a shooting star they are beautiful and then disappear like an exhale on a cold day. I live for these deep encounters. Even as a child I knew that something magical was there waiting for an event that would annihilate the darkness and bring back the brilliance of that place.

I'm still waiting for that cosmic Event, but now I know what I'm waiting for and I know what it is that Haunts me.

I have felt the presence of the One my heart desires.

Looking into that deep dark chasm my eyes are mostly blind. And without steady light or sure footing–darkness can be crippling. It's hard to keep walking into the unknown. Yet, even as a child, I would not surrender to the fear that Darkness tried to use to keep me from coming closer.

The emptiness, the sadness, the darkness was what I needed to step into in order to discover what was missing. I believe the stepping is a process called *living*.

I believe it's called responding to desire – no matter what the outcome.

And if Evil could keep me from coming into contact with the consequences of living I just might escape falling into the abyss. If he could lead me around the void he could keep me from true life and from my ultimate Desire.

Throughout the course of my life Evil has done everything it could to get me to surrender to a safe, comfortable and predictable life lived in denial or avoidance.

There were a plethora of tips and tricks on how to avoid the void. And enough half-truths to deny it's existence. To make an agreement with Denial or Avoidance and avoid or deny that there is a void – a chasm . . . to deny the music I hear coming from somewhere out there would have catastrophic consequences. Both Good and Evil knew that.

The more I walked into that void the more Evil hunted me down. But as I walked the louder and more frequent the music, the warm wind, the glimpses of light or the caress of the warm breeze became.

The memories got more haunting. The last thing Evil wanted me to do was to feel the pull of Destiny.

He tried building a steeple-like structure over the abyss to hide it and when I heard music from the underside of the floor beneath the pew I fidgeted in, I became curious and much to the annoyance of all the varicose-veined legs around me I began my search on my knees under the pews for whence it came.

Denial, Fear, Resignation, Shame, Guilt, Parental Scorn, Religiosity none of those demons got a solid footing on my heart, though my mind may have tried to make agreements with them at different times in my life–my heart literally wouldn't let me.

My heart was compelled to believe that there was something I had to have in that void. And I let my heart lead the way. Though it had every reason in the world to shut out the pain of life and retreat. Instead, to my heart, the void seemed to be a passage to a better place.

Something existed there in that passageway that was my destiny and nothing and nobody was going to keep me from it.

I must have frustrated the hell out of Evil for he could not lure me with his artificial sunshine into permanent residence around his chilly campfire.

I could not deny the void. Never. Nothing in me was strong enough to ignore it and pretend it wasn't there. Nothing in me was able to embrace the glow of the cold campfire on the edges of religiosity when I felt the warmth calling to me from within the darkness.

God gave us other senses that take over when our eyes can not see–if we will but let them. And those other senses have been my lifeline.

So, I close my eyes and let my heart follow what I heard or felt. In so doing, I've been drawn into the dark by a force that I have surrendered to. Love. Desire. Longing. They have called to me through the darkness. And as I walk into the dark – responding to my other senses – I see.

My other senses take over. And it is from there that I've realized that what I have felt was the touch of him who used to walk the halls of my heart with me–hand in hand–as lovers do. His whispers to me part the darkness for a moment in time.

The love my human heart remembers has become the hope I cling to. The image my Creator put there.

So I wait very impatiently for the moment when the darkness will disappear to be replaced with something unimaginable. Something incredible. Something that words will not be able to describe.

What I know to be true about the void has grown and fully embraced me. I'm too deep in the passageway of that void to ever go back. The movement is not reversible. I feel the pain of the darkness so much because I know what used to live there was not darkness at all, but light and love.

Haunted? Yes, I would say that I was haunted in the best of ways by what once was and what will be again. Living with that void throughout my life has not dis-heartened me, but it has kept me alive.

That void has revealed my desire for the One. And it has driven me towards complete madness. A craving I can't satisfy. Irrational movements that I can't explain. A splinter in my mind. A way of seeing. A love I can not deny. A rhythm only I hear. And it is good.

What is in the void? It is the unfulfilled desire left in me by the One who will return for me.

All my life I have waited for my moment. The moment I meet my Destiny. The moment when my destiny is complete: My first night with the King.

INTO THE VOID

This is what I see when I stare into the void left by him whom I love . . .

The darkness reveals itself as two tall doors standing before me. On the other side of those doors I know there to be a light that my body has longed to bathe in. Something amazing is longing to take my breath away.

I'm not completely sure what that will be but the sensual scent of forever wafts under the door. It is an aroma that awakens my senses and quickens my heartbeat. Through the cracks around the door I can hear music playing and every-once-in-awhile I hear the voice that I've heard all my life. He calls my name and through the thick, disheartening doors I can hear his words of love for me fading in and out. I can hear his frustration with the door that has been forced between us. Deep and enchanting–he talks directly to me and I have begun to be able to hear him more and more.

I long to see the eyes behind the voice and be captured by them. I know his heart. He is a Warrior. He is a King. He is my Love. And he is Good. But I still do not feel his skin on mine. The desire for the touch of him on my skin makes the void so much deeper.

All of me wants to be one with him.

I want to melt into him. I want to invite him into me and give him my beauty. I want to feel his strength upon me. He is the other half that makes me whole–the man of my dreams. My destiny. I just want our eyes to lock onto each other and I want to melt into his strong embrace. Like a romantic novel, he is the hero and I am the one he pursues. I long to hear with my own ears and see with my own eyes the words, "Will you be Mine?" come out of his mouth.

The deepest desire that I am aware of is my desire to be on the other side of those doors and be embraced by the one who owns that voice.

To finally experience my imagination surrender to reality. The reflections I've seen of him are not enough anymore! I wish those damn doors would just fly open so I could hear and see him clearly. He has become so enticing to me that I can not hold back my love.

Our love has become what I live for. My heart has done what it wants to. It has gone where it wants to. I can not stop it–even if I wanted to I could not.

I am in love. And I have fallen hard.

Logic and common sense have been replaced with a romance of 'against all odds,' 'wishing upon a star' and 'once upon a time.' And so I live with those doors ever before me, waiting and dreaming of what lies beyond them. I will be there the moment those doors open. And when they do I will never be the same again.

It is to what I know to be on the other side of that door to which I am drawn and the reason I live . . .

THE DOORS OPEN

I have been preparing for and longing for this moment all my life. The moment those doors open I shall meet my destiny.

I hear shouting from the other side. There is much commotion. Happiness. Excitement. I hear his voice louder and louder. I hear banging on the door.

With strong hands it is unbolted. The hinges, unused for thousands of years, begin to creak open. And then, what my heart has been denied since the fall of man begins to happen. The veil between mortal and immortal begins to dematerialize. Those doors gradually begin to crack open. My heart beats faster. My new reality–the one that I remember–begins to seep into my heart. I will not perish on the dark side of these doors. For real!

I am nervous, but it is far too late for the questions of: *Am I pretty enough? Am I ready to meet him? Will he be pleased? Will he really be on the other side of that door?* The questions disappear into the blackness behind me and my eyes are fixated on the light coming from the edges of my hell.

Forward is the only movement to make.

My mind is too weak to fathom this moment, but my heart is recording every moment. It knows I am here. My heart has been longing for this forever and finally I am beginning to encounter the coming of the King–*for me!*

As the doors persist in opening into the expanse of my dark night, the bright light streams through the cracks. Too much for my humanity, the dazzling light that streams out from this gateway into eternity, forces me to quickly put my hands up to my face and cover my eyes or I know I will die or go blind.

The darkness is abandoned and surrenders to the brilliance of forever. It is that immortal and resplendent moment I've been waiting for all my life, yet I find out that there is a fine line between excitement and terror. And so I stand unable to move . . . yet.

As those massive doors–my companion for years–open wider, the light finds me–no longer in darkness–but never-the-less still outside the doors. But now I'm standing in the pathway of the light, as if I am on stage with a spotlight upon me.

Whatever glories lay in that light I know I am not dressed for. My hair is in knots from the raging winds of the dark. My dress has been torn from escaping the clutches of thugs sent by Evil to hunt me down. I have been violated and hidden lace has been ripped from me. The dark passage of shadows has taken its toll on me. Traveling through dense thickets in the night has left my skin torn up and scars all over me. My body is bruised and bloody from close encounters with the rugged terrain that I crawled through to get to this door.

All-in-all I look like I've been through hell and I am in no way presentable to *the* King. My heart is prepared to meet him, but at that moment I find myself very unprepared to approach the love of my life for the first time.

But what wonders! Those feelings of my reality do not even get to settle in my heart before something right out of a fairy-tale begins to happen to . . . *me*.

The light seems to awaken to my desire and begins to encircle me. As if the light is alive, it surrounds me and explodes into flickering magical stars. Like the stars that encircled Cinderella, I watch them travel up my legs and around my body. In glorious fairy-tale fashion they sparkle and dance around me to the music I hear coming from inside of forever. The stars that envelop my body seem happy and in a twinkling of an eye my body begins to change.

I twirl around and feel the tingle of newness in every inch of my being. I feel a new life flow through my veins–strong and immortal. I feel my skin soft and new. The features on my face change and all imperfections become replaced with alluring beauty.

All of my senses are heightened and everything is more than it was. I feel soft, thick hair falling down my back and over my shoulders. I feel taller and the affliction of gravity seems to have lifted. I'm enchanted by the delightful scents wafting around me. My lungs draw-in air like they have never inhaled before and I feel the penetrating oxygen circulate through my body.

As the stars make their way up my body I gaze upon my form in the reflection they make. Lovely. A form to enchant the gods, draped in linen so sheer one can not wonder–an invitation to enter. The imperfect body that has beset my life–now gone. Something has fallen away from my eyes and the darkness that once plagued my life suddenly disappears and I begin to see my mythical reality as it truly is. The physical battle wounds that I have endured in the darkness disappear and the light transforms my flesh into a beauty I have always dreamed of. The stars trigger an explosion of events and from them emerge a beauty on my outside that matches the beauty he wrote on my heart.

Walking on into the flickering light of thousands of stars, I'm almost pulled through those two tall doors that open before me. My eyes adjust to the interior of a majestic hall–the one I've dreamed about and seen in my head for years.

Tall columns made of marble line the edges of the courtroom. Candles flicker everywhere and the most stirring music that fits the movement of my heart is playing skillfully from somewhere unseen. The hall is filled with thousands of beings . . . yet all I can see is him.

And then I was there, within just two arms'
length of him. Everything else fell away–
the presence of the thousands around us,
the splendor of our surroundings, the
grandness of the occasion. All that existed
were his eyes, which bore into mine with a
fire that seemed to warm every inch of my
body. Despite my wish to maintain a regal
expression, I could not help but shyly smile
again at the sight of him. I tried to kneel,
but he took my hand and raised me up at
once. He spoke in a low, intimate voice, as
though all the others did not exist.*

And then I melted into his smile, felt his skin upon mine and I heard his voice upon my neck, *Welcome, Lady Mithril. You are a rare beauty indeed, a treasure worth more than all the stars combined. I've longed for you to be here with me. Up to one-half of the Kingdom is yours. Ask anything and I will give it to you. What is your wish?*

Without a hesitation I whisper into his ear, "My only wish is to have your heart," and after I exhale those words I breath in the scent of Royalty, of a King, of a new family–of my Knight.

This is what I see. This is the fabric of who I am. I was born for The Dance. I was born to live with the void at the center of who I am–for now. Not put there by him who loves

---

* <u>One Night with the King</u>, Tommy Tenny, page 296

me, but a consequence of a fallen world. Yet a consequence I have embraced for it has had a profound effect on my salvation and my sight.

He has captured my heart. It is Him that I see. It is Him that I come to. It is Him who I want to give myself to. It is his heart that I desire.

That is all I want. His heart. The King of the Universe in love with me? The Mightiest of Warriors in my embrace? What is it about this Lover that pulls me towards him? Do I dare hope for it? Do I dare dream of such a moment?

All my life this desire has deepened in me until I can no longer separate it from myself.

This is who I am. There is nothing deeper than this.

Opposite page: Mithril (Rebekah Garvin)

THE WEALTH OF MORIA

(Your song) . . . 'makes the darkness seem heavier, thinking of all those lamps in your song. Are there piles of jewels and gold lyin g about here still?'

Gimli was silent. Having sung his song he would say no more.

'Piles of jewels? said Gandalf. 'No. The Orcs have often plundered Moria; there is nothing left in the upper halls. And since the dwarves fled, no one dares to seek the shafts and treasuries down in the deep places: they are drowned in water of in a shadow of fear.'

'Then what do the dwarves want to come back for?" asked Sam.

'For *mithril*,' answered Gandalf.
'The wealth of Moria was not in
gold and jewels, the toys of the
the Dwarves; nor in iron, their
servant. Such things they found
here, it is true, expecially iron;
but they did not need to delve for
them: all things that they desired
they could obtain in traffic. For
here alone in the world was found
Moria-silver, or true-silver as
some have called it: *mithril* is
the Elvish name. The Dwarves have
a name which they do not tell. It's
worth is ten times that of gold,
and now it is beyond price; for
little is left above the ground,
and even the Orcs dare not delve
here for it . . .

'*Mithril!* All folk desired it.
It could be beaten like copper,
and polished like glass; and the
Dwarves could make of it a metal,
light and yet harder than tempered
steel. It's beauty was like to that
of common silver, but the beauty
of mithril did not tarnish or grow
dim. The Elves dearly loved it,

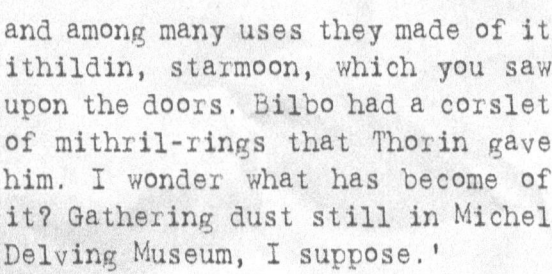

and among many uses they made of it
ithildin, starmoon, which you saw
upon the doors. Bilbo had a corslet
of mithril-rings that Thorin gave
him. I wonder what has become of
it? Gathering dust still in Michel
Delving Museum, I suppose.'

'What?' cried Gimli, startled
out of his silence. 'A corselt of
Moria-silver? That was a kingly
gift!'

'Yes,' said Gandalf. 'I never told
him, but its worth was greater
than the value of the whole Shire
and everything in it.'

Frodo said nothing, but he put his
hand under this tunic and touched
the rings of his mail-shirt. He
felt staggered to think that he had
been walking about with the price
of the Shire under his jacket. Had
Bilbo known? He felt no doubt that
Bilbo knew quite well.

It was indeed a kingly gift.

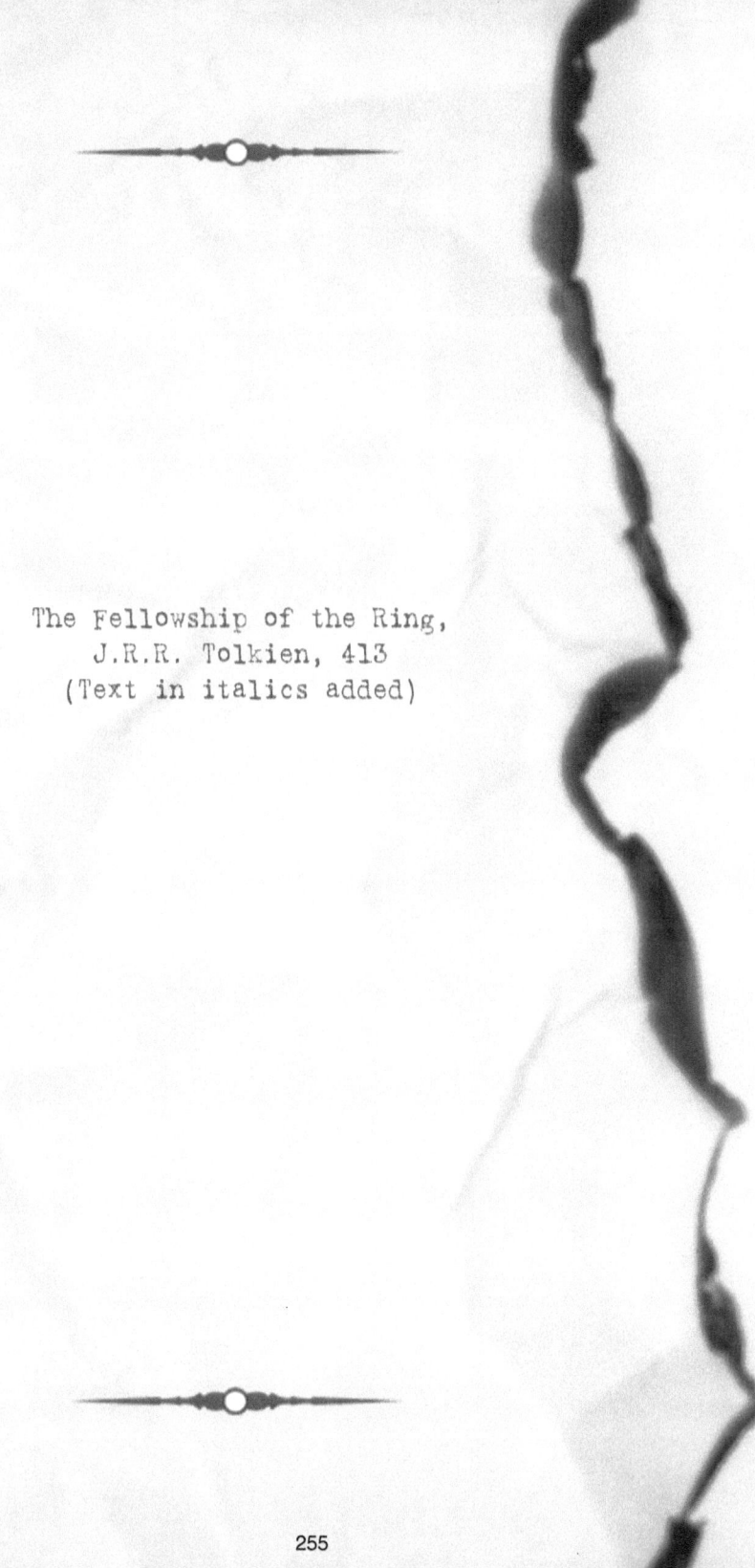

The Fellowship of the Ring,
J.R.R. Tolkien, 413
(Text in italics added)

✿ ✿ ✿

THE BELOVED'S PRAYER

by Jan Finnamore

A few years ago, I sensed God was urging me to pray The Daily Prayer every day. At first, I found this to be difficult. I soon discovered that even though I had grown up in Christianity, I did not understand what the prayer meant at all. And often as I would force myself to pray it, I would have to fight extreme sleepiness even though I had just had a good night's sleep. Other times, I could hardly make my mouth form the words. I pressed on, but it felt mechanical, and my mind insisted on wandering...it seemed like it took forever to get through it. In an attempt at understanding, I looked up every Scripture reference hoping to find some spark of life, yet still the prayer was exhausting and dead to me. But stronger still, was the hunch that I was being blocked from the richness of the prayer, so I forced myself to stay with it and I pressed on day after day

Finally, I started asking God, "What does this mean? What do you want me to know here?" And bit by bit He started to show me. Piece by piece He opened the eyes of my understanding. And as each part came alive to me I scribbled notes in my book on the pages of the prayer, so that I wouldn't lose what God had just shown me. One day, I realized I was praying it with joy and strength and entering into the depth of what it truly meant for me. It was now something I looked forward to everyday. After a few months, I realized that I had it memorized and could pray through all of it (or even just a random phrase from it) anywhere I was (at a stoplight, while washing dishes...etc.) anywhere I was battling and needing to remember who I was in Christ, or what God's heart toward me was.

I love The Daily Prayer and pray it often still. It is a friend and has played a significant part in my journey.

This past summer, as part of that journey, I sensed God was wanting me to write my own freedom fighting prayer...to find my own voice. I was a little daunted by the task, but I asked God to give me the words, and in the process He ministered great healing to my heart.

I offer The Beloved's Prayer below, not to replace The Daily Prayer, but to encourage you to dive into The Daily Prayer if you haven't yet--to encourage you to press past any fog that you may encounter there. It is a treasure. Through it, God took me deeper into who I am in Him, and gave me my own words to express my love and freedom in Him.

My Dear Yeshua, I come to you today to agree with you about all that you see in me and long for me to be. I come to you today to reclaim my heart, to join you in your rescue and restoration of it. To stand my ground against the enemy's plans to harm it and to claim all that is rightfully mine that you won for me through your complete work on the cross, in your resurrection and in the fullness of your ascension. I come to clear my vision, to see the view from Mount Zion, to see things as you see them, for I am indeed seated in the heavenlies with you.

Beloved Father, I come to you asking for forgiveness for the ways I have not counted on your love, for the ways I have hurt your heart, hurt the kingdom and hurt those you love. Reveal those things to me, help me to see them as you see them so that I may run from the ways of death and embrace the way of love and life instead. Forgive me for the glory I have caused you to miss. Search me by your Spirit. Cleanse me by your Son's blood. Take pity on me; remember my frame of dust, my struggle with the flesh and have mercy on me and heal me. Bring me to wholeness. I crucify my flesh and impale it to Christ's cross, and declare myself hidden with Christ in God. I surrender to the Spirit's healing and restorative work on my behalf. I rest in the knowledge of your love for me and your promise of working all things out for me. I stand upright, robed in righteousness receiving your full pardon and forgiveness. I renounce the Lie of Nothingness–that nothing good is happening and that all will end badly. I make no agreements with it. I choose to walk instead in the confidence that you are actively working all things together for good on my behalf. I choose to walk in step with you, Lord, and to not run ahead and create my own light.

I put on the full armor of God. The armor you wear, God of the Angel Armies is armor fit for me as well. I put on your truth, may it speak louder than any lie. I put on your righteousness, knowing that it is mine in Christ. I put on your salvation, knowing that I have been saved, I am being saved and I will be fully saved. I raise up faith as a canopy of protection for me, choosing to believe that you are good no matter what it may look like at any given moment. I choose to wield your Word as a powerful weapon against every lie launched against me. I choose to pray in the Spirit. And I choose to walk along side you in preparing and bringing the good news that brings peace. I choose to wear the crowns you gave mankind at creation that were lost to us, but have now been regained through Christ--the crowns of glory, dominion and fruitfulness.

Jehovah, God of the Angel Armies, I ask you to send out battalions of your warrior angels to war and to work on my behalf. May they guard me and all within my domain this day. Lord, show me by your Spirit any points of entry, any weak places the enemy may use to gain entrance. Show me any agreements I have made with the darkness, any lies I have been naive in believing, any lies lodged deeply within me from my past. Bring those lies to the surface, speak your sentences of truth and love to every place. Lord, I come under your covenant promise that I will not be destroyed and I believe that your covenant promise is a hiding place of protection for me. Your rainbow banner over me is love. I bring my family and all that are within my domain under your banner of love this day.

Thank you for your great love, Trinity. If you are for me, who can be against me? And you are for me, finishing the beautiful work you started in me. So I praise you, Great Fellowship of Hearts for your care and complete provision for me. Thank you for inviting me to dine with you at your table of delights. Thank you for inviting me to dance and to play. Thank you for inviting me to war and to rule and extend your domain. Holy Spirit, increase my longing for my Groom. Make me desperately hungry and thirsty for the Living Word. Increase my ability to hear your voice and see your hand. Open the eyes of my heart. Prompt my heart to praise and adoration in the moments of this day. Take me to the next step. Protect me in the battle. Heighten my awareness of evil. Keep my feet from slipping. Bring me into the fullness of the knowledge of your great love. And as you will, bring me into my glory so that I might most beautifully glorify you. Open the windows of heaven and bless me indeed.

Thank you that your hand of favor rests upon my head. Thank you that you are within me, here in the moments, now and for always. Thank you that you have blessed me with all of the blessings of the heavenly realm in Christ and that I can walk in confidence of your good heart toward me. I love you, LORD, for I am yours and you are mine. These things I ask Father, Son and Holy Spirit with the full backing and authority of Yeshua's name.

– Your Bride, your Beloved –

Come for my heart, Jesus. Find me!

❦ ❦ ❦

THANK-YOU

As I worked on this book, designing it and laying it out, I *soaked* in your stories. It was hard not to. I was ever curious as to what the next story would bring. It was as if I was walking through the remains of a burnt down castle and was unearthing gold coins, chains, silver platters and old photos. Each one holding an amazing story of it's own. Sacred ground. Stunning.

What we have stumbled upon is a strong box of loot. Kingdom loot. Kingdom treasure. And there is so much more to unearth.

I'm so glad that you have let me and the world into your lives! Thank-you for being authentic and transparent. Thank you for taking the time to share the transformation that God has done and is doing on your hearts. The common thread through-out all our stories is clear . . . the Mightiest Warrior of them all is on a final move towards setting the captives free. Aslan is on the move.

Thank you, John Eldredge and your team for providing the words that have helped unlock our hearts so that God's Holy Spirit could take us on a new journey towards abundant life and the restoration of our hearts. His heart towards me has become revealed through your wisdom, words and walk.

To The Kingdom and to The Warring Trinity,
Rebekah Garvin

The **Land of Iona** is a collective redemptive community of like-hearts in allied relationship with The Trinity in the Kingdom of Light. The Land's website is currently being developed with the goal of uniting the Body for synergy—the simultaneous action of separate agencies which, together, have greater total effect than the sum of their individual effects. It is a place where the Bride can connect with each other, live, share, and work together—advancing the Kingdom of God.

We envision the site becoming a hub of a mythical Round Table of Knights whom God has gathered from every corner of the Kingdom. Each having experienced the freedom Jesus offers; each walking in their own individual journeys and God given strengths; each rising to the glory of their calling and stature, yet all uniting together for greater total effect...just as it took all of the clans coming together to free Scotland.

In its broadest sense, Iona is the Body, the true Bride of Christ. When we refer to Iona, we are meaning all who have ever engaged with God to be a part of this mythical Iona–from ages past to ages to come. Only God knows all of whom are or have been part of Iona. Kingdoms of all sizes have, do and will exist within Iona. As part of the larger community of believers the people within these kingdoms live life together, fight for each other and are of one heart. Instead of the traditional hierarchies and questing after the approval of man, the Land of Iona will be self-governed and launched upon a belief that our hearts, living under the new covenant, are good.

The Land of Iona is a place where we are invited to join other awakened hearts, live in The Message of the Heart and walk in the Four Streams. Together we will draw the world up into our mythical reality, Great Story, and into the heart of our King–the Mystical One–the Amazing Trinity.

Engage with us and create an alliance with the other hearts developing this site by adding your art skills, web development skills or finances to make this huge project a reality.

Visit the site at **www.landofiona.com** to create an alliance, to browse, to find events, and to register in the Land. As time goes by there will be many other things that will evolve there. Engage with us and discover a place to offer the weight of your life, find others who have gotten to know God's true identity, and journey into like-hearted fellowship we all crave.

A BIT ABOUT US

Jan and Rebekah are a testimony to the fact that like-hearts can be brought together over the miles. For they have actually never met each other in person, but have worked together on not only this book but the Friends of Ransomed Heart website and the Land of Iona website and have grown close in spirit.

Jan Finnamore is the author of *Captive Heart--Love's Story*. Rebekah Garvin is the author of *Conversations with our Kindergartner* and her thoughts are included in the book *Notes from the Road, Vol. 1*.

Jan Finnamore lives in Currier & Ives New England with her husband Curt and their two children. When Jan is not washing dishes, you may find her in the hammock surrounded by flower beds down by the river, or on a long walk with her children along tree-canopied streets winding to sugar houses and covered bridges. She is passionate about helping hearts come to know God as a Lover who rescues and restores.

Rebekah Garvin lives in North Idaho with her husband Chris and their two children. Though many things require her time, Rebekah likes to be known as one who walks with God–intimatly. Waterskiing, harvesting and sunbathing are three of her many passions. While her husband is currently pursuing a Master's Degree in Counseling, Rebekah can be found on the ice-rink pursing a figure skating dream. Rebekah owns A Chance Encounter (a graphic design/photography studio) and Starlight Publishing. She also loves to speak, write and direct dramas.

STARLIGHT PUBLISHING

www.lulu.com/starlight

Starlight Publishing is a small publishing company that seeks to print books revealing the hope of true Christianity and the offer of Jesus for freedom and the restoration of our hearts. We desire our readers to enter into the Sacred Romance with the amazing Trinity. May our books be a spark that lights the flame in your soul!

Our books are printed on demand through Lulu. For consideration of your manuscript, layout and design pricing contact Starlight Publishing through the mail: PMB 173; 2900 Government Way; Coeur d'Alene, Idaho 83815 or by email: rebekah@achanceencounter.net.

If you have a story to contribute
to *Ransomed Hearts–Our Story,* we'd be happy to
consider it for a future volume.

Contact us by email through the Land of Iona at:
support@landofiona.com.

www.ingramcontent.com/pod-product-compliance
Lightning Source LLC
Chambersburg PA
CBHW022005010726
47494CB00003B/897

* 9 7 8 0 6 1 5 1 4 5 6 2 4 *